BRAC PACK

Keata's F
George's ˌurn

Lynn Hagen

**EVERLASTING CLASSIC
MANLOVE**

Siren Publishing, Inc.
www.SirenPublishing.com

A SIREN PUBLISHING BOOK
IMPRINT: Everlasting Classic ManLove

BRAC PACK, VOLUME 4
Keata's Promise
George's Turn
Copyright © 2011 by Lynn Hagen

ISBN-10: 1-61034-658-0
ISBN-13: 978-1-61034-658-0

First Printing: June 2011

Cover design by Jinger Heaston
All art and logo copyright © 2011 by Siren Publishing, Inc.

Printed in the U.S.A.

PUBLISHER
Siren Publishing, Inc.
www.SirenPublishing.com

DEDICATIONS

Keata's Promise

To my children who are grown now but still love to play pranks on each other.

George's Turn

To all the Georges out there. May you find your Tank.

SIREN
Publishing

KEATA'S PROMISE

LYNN HAGEN

Everlasting Classic

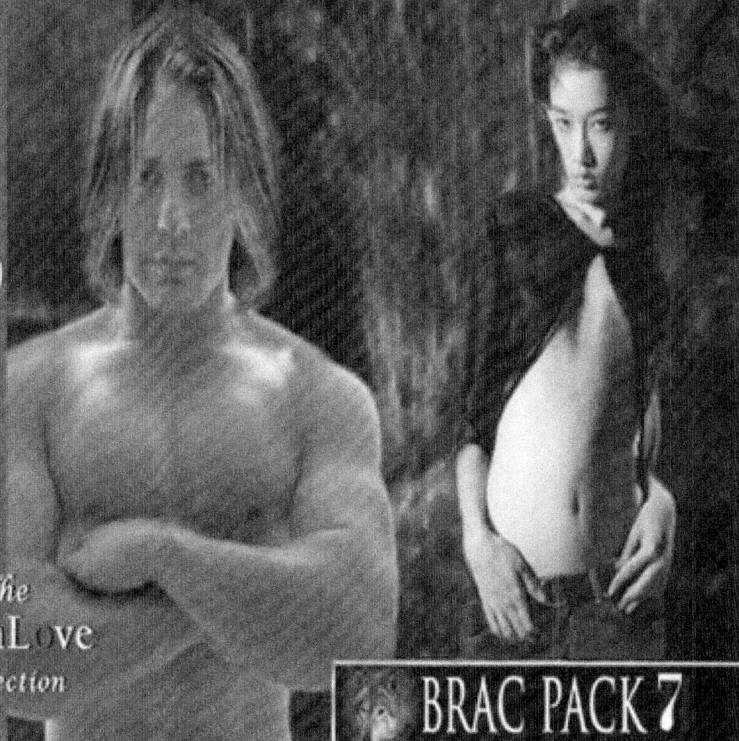

The
ManLove
Collection

BRAC PACK 7

KEATA'S PROMISE

Brac Pack 7

LYNN HAGEN
Copyright © 2011

Chapter One

Keata and Johnny raced through the halls, Micah hot on their heels.

They rounded the corner and flew through Keata's bedroom door, slamming it shut and locking it.

"That was funny." Johnny fell on the floor laughing.

Keata giggled right along with him. "You see face?"

"Priceless. I can't help it he doesn't find it funny to have mayonnaise on his pie instead of whipped cream." He laughed louder.

"It was good prank," Keata agreed. "Hey, who took book?"

"What book?" Johnny pushed up from the floor.

Keata tried to remember where he put his book. It wasn't by his bed where he remembered leaving it. "My book I leave by bed."

"I'll help you look for it."

They searched the whole room, but it was nowhere to be found. Maybe he took it downstairs to the den.

"I leave right there." Keata pointed to his nightstand.

"Did you let someone borrow it?" Johnny asked as he searched under the bed.

Keata plopped on the floor and threw his hands into the air. "Who can read?"

"Good point."

Just because he didn't remember taking it out of the room didn't mean he hadn't. Keata often did things without thought only to think about it later—sometimes too late when his butt was already in trouble.

He opened the dresser drawers and tossed his clothes around, some landing on the floor as he looked for the precious books Oliver had given him. Scratching his head, Keata spun around looking at the mess on the floor, hoping he had overlooked it.

"I'm not cleaning that up." Johnny pointed to the mess.

There was nothing but jeans and underwear thrown about.

He got on all fours as he looked under nightstand. No dang book! Keata was getting frustrated the longer he had to look.

"My stupid luck, I not find book," he said to Johnny as he huffed.

His thoughts wandered to Japan and his life there as they searched his closet, tossing everything off of the shelves.

His cousin Kyoshi had rescued him more times than he could count. He had always trusted what people told him and blindly followed. Nine times out of ten he ended up regretting it. Keata couldn't help it. People should be honest like him. Maybe because he had desperately wanted friends he jumped in feetfirst before really thinking it through. The people back home in Japan never really wanted to be his friend. They wanted to pick on the naïve Keata, the trusting Keata, and the girly looking Keata.

Keata knew this, yet he still trusted people, hoping that one of those bullies would want to be friends. He wished that one of them would feel bad for what they did and see Keata as more than an easy target.

Not a one did. They all treated him like a guy they could push around. They would laugh and taunt him. Some even threw him to the ground. This angered Keata. Just because they said he was different didn't give them a right to treat him that way.

"We could look downstairs," Johnny suggested.

"Hope Micah gone." Keata cracked the door open and peeked out. The hall was clear, so he and Johnny left the room.

Keata held the banister as he walked down the winding staircase, thinking of the new friends he had. He could trust them. They made him feel like he belonged. His favorite friend was Johnny, of course. They thought alike, simply. Johnny was a human mated to a wolf warrior named Hawk. Now, Hawk was one scary man. He looked like he could break your bones just with one stare, and that's why Keata liked him.

"You see my book?" he asked Blair who was walking toward the den.

"Sorry, buddy."

Keata and Johnny veered toward the den with Blair. He started thinking about Kysohi.

Keata remembered how he and his cousin, Kyoshi, had been taken from the streets of Japan and stuffed in a box. Kyoshi had called it a cargo box. It sailed across the ocean and brought them to America where big ugly Americans tried to steal them.

Kyoshi escaped with Keata, and they ended up here. He had been homesick for awhile. Everything was so strange and different from where he grew up. He still struggled to communicate with the people who lived in this big house.

"All people stop." Keata put up his hands. Drew, Blair, Oliver, and Cecil froze, not one finger moved.

Keata rolled his eyes, the small men here always joked.

"I need to find book."

"Is it due back at the library?" Cecil chuckled.

"No, but someone take from me." Keata narrowed his eyes at the troublemaker of the group.

"Fine." Cecil threw his hands up, and they all began to search the den.

"Hey, I found some gum." Drew held the pack up.

"I found a quarter and...*eww.*" Blair dropped whatever it was, and it hit the floor.

Keata wrinkled his nose. It was hairy and black. Yuck.

When the search yielded no results—besides coins and candy—Keata balled his fists up in frustration.

The other men left, but Keata kept searching, his thoughts getting lost again.

One of the mates, Oliver, had suggested that Kyoshi teach them all Japanese. It helped a lot, but he still had trouble at times understanding them.

Keata was so absorbed in his thoughts, he hadn't even seen his friend Tank shooting pool with a wolf named Murdock. Keata thought a lot of them had funny names. He knew all the big men were wolves, the smaller ones their mates. He really didn't understand what a mate was.

Kyoshi tried over and over again to explain it to him. He knew it meant the people who were mates were boyfriends. No one else could have them. Keata also knew it meant that they kissed a lot and touched each other. That was about as much as he knew on the subject of mates.

"Hey, buddy. What's up?"

Keata smiled at Tank.

"I lost my book." Keata searched the couches and behind the bar again. The den was set up nicely. There were two suede sofas, a large screen television, a pool table, full bar, a dart board, a poker table and Cecil's video game.

"Will you help me?"

"Anything for you, Keata."

Tank helped him search, but they came up empty-handed, just like the first time. Where could he have put it? He racked his brain, trying to remember the last place he had it. The mate, Oliver, had bought him mangas written in Japanese. He would be devastated if he couldn't find it.

He kicked the couch in anger.

"Better watch it. It kicks back." Tank chuckled

Keata blew a raspberry at Tank and plopped down on the couch, crossing his arms over his chest.

He wasn't fluent in English like Kyoshi was, so the books were more comforting than anything else. They had good stories, too.

"You want to go into town?" Tank asked as he looked under the couches, lifting it off of the floor while Keata sat on it.

Keata held on, thinking how strong Tank must be to do that. Keata was only five two. Tank was at least six seven. Keata knew the warrior weighed over three hundred pounds because he heard the other mates say so. Tank was bulging with muscles. "You better not drop," Keata warned.

Tank laughed and sat the couch down. "Now would I do that to you?"

His dark brown eyes always twinkled when he smiled at Keata.

His brown hair was cut really low, and Keata liked it. It was different from his long black hair. The kids back in Japan used to laugh at him and say he looked like a girl. Keata didn't think he looked like a girl, but if everyone said so, he must.

"Okay, Tank, I go with you, but I find book first." Keata visited the kitchen next. He remembered coming in here last night for a snack. Maybe he left it on the table. Keata saw that the table was empty. He tried the fridge just to make sure he hadn't sat it in there when he got his juice. No book. But there was plenty of juice left. Keata grabbed a bottle and drank his fill, placing the cap back on it for later. He sat in on the table and started to wonder if he ever had a book.

It couldn't have just disappeared, could it?

"Hey, Keata."

Keata looked over his shoulder to see Cody. This wolf was always nice to him. He didn't talk much to Keata, but he was always watching him. Whenever he saw that Keata noticed him staring, he would quickly walk away.

The wolf was strange that way.

"Hi, Cody, you see my book?" Keata checked the pantry. He could have left it there when he took some crackers last night.

"No book. Sorry."

When Cody did speak, he always tried to make it simple. Keata liked that. It made talking to him easy. He always got a strange flutter in his stomach around Cody, like an invisible string pulled on his belly button trying to make him go to the wolf. No matter how many times he tried, Cody always ran away before he got close enough.

He knew that Cody was boyfriends with the wolf with red hair named Jasper.

Keata stood by the counter, staring at the warrior. He had never seen hair with every color in it before. It was hip—using Oliver's word—and his brown eyes reminded Keata of a chocolate. He thought Cody a very handsome wolf.

"How are you feeling? Your leg?" Cody leaned against the doorframe, watching Keata. He did that a lot. Keata rubbed his hands on his pant legs. Anytime the wolf was around, he sweated a lot. Keata didn't understand the swirly emotions that always messed with his belly when he looked at Cody.

"Leg good. It no hurt." Keata slowly moved toward Cody, wanting to bridge the gap, but for every step forward he took, the wolf took one back. Confused, he moved out of the kitchen and back up the stairs to his room.

"I lose my mind here." Keata shook his head in confused frustration

Since he didn't understand the feelings he had for Cody, he pushed them aside as he lay on his bed. Maybe he would go find Tank and go into town with him. Tank always made sure he had fun. He didn't have swirly feeling for the wolf Tank, just a warm friendship feeling.

"You feeling okay?" Kyoshi asked as he entered Keata's room.

"Lemon peachy." Keata gave him a thumbs-up.

"Liar." Kyoshi pushed him aside and sat on the bed. "Now tell me what's eating you."

"Brain cells."

"Oookay. Just as long as no one is bothering you." Kyoshi gave him that knowing look.

Keata was *not* about to get into yet another debate with Kyoshi about the wolves in this house. He was tired of his cousin interrogating the warriors about being too close to him.

"You live down hall. I get you if need to." Keata rolled over and gave Kyoshi his back, telling his cousin he was through talking.

Kyoshi patted his leg and stood, sighing deeply as he left.

Deciding he would go with Tank, he changed into something warm then went looking for the large wolf. He found him in Alpha Maverick's office talking with the tallest wolf he had ever seen. Maverick reminded Keata of a gentle giant. He stood almost as tall as the office door but always spoke softly to Keata and answered all his questions the best he could. He liked Maverick. He waved at the Alpha shyly like he always did, and Maverick smiled and waved back like he always did.

* * * *

"I go with you, Tank?" Keata asked when Tank stopped talking and looked in his direction.

"You go, Keata." Tank smiled and excused himself.

"Come on, Keata. We can go." Tank led him out to his half-ton truck. Being three hundred and twenty pounds, Tank needed a super duty truck. He helped the pint-size guy in and buckled his seat belt, scanning the area for any sign of intruders. He didn't need a repeat of what had happened to the Sentry Micah.

Micah had taken his mate, Oliver, out to dinner, inviting Keata to tag along. On their way home, they were run off the road by rogue wolves and Keata had been attacked, his thigh bitten into, leaving a nasty scar behind.

Tank had fought for Keata when he was told by his Alpha they were under attack. Keata meant the world to the Sentries. He was young and naïve, beautiful to the point of looking androgynous. They all took it upon themselves to look out for him and keep him out of trouble because Keata was very inquisitive and friendly. Too damn trusting in Tank's opinion.

"You can pick the music." Tank pointed to the radio.

Keata beamed and began to play with the dials.

"No way, Keata." Tank growled when Keata left it on a country station.

"I like."

"No way, change it."

"Then why tell me I pick?" He pouted.

"Pick anything but that." There was no way he was listening to country.

"Fine." Keata began to mess with the dials again, picking a rock station.

"Now you're talking." He laughed. "Give me some dap."

"What dap?"

"Ball your fist up and give it to me."

Keata did and Tank tapped it with his knuckles.

"Hip." He giggled.

"Very."

Keata's stomach grumbled loud enough that it was heard over the music.

"Are you hungry?" Tank asked as they pulled into a parking spot close to the diner. Tank had to pick some things up from the post office, and the diner was only right next door. In a small town, everything was in walking distant once you were in the town square.

Brac Village was the perfect place to live in Tank's opinion.

"Little. I can get smoothie?" Keata beamed up at him.

"Anything my little friend wants." Tank held the truck door open as Keata hopped down and started toward the diner.

"Hold on, Keata. You know to wait for me." The Sentries had entertained the thought of getting one of those human kid leashes for Keata. The guy wandered everywhere and would disappear in five seconds flat, claiming something sparkly had caught his eye. Tank loved the wonderment in Keata, but it made for a solid headache when they had to chase him down.

"Sorry, Tank." Keata took Tank's hand as they made their way into the diner. It wasn't that Keata was too young—he was eighteen years old. He was just unaccustomed to the ways of America and didn't see the dangers in wandering around alone. Again, he was too damn trusting and would wander off with a stranger in a heartbeat to go look for a nonexistent puppy. The Sentries took no chances with Keata.

They grabbed a booth by the window, and Tank tried to explain the menu. Kyoshi had been working with Keata on American food, the names and combinational ways to eat them. Keata seemed keen on chicken strips and fries along with smoothies.

"You find your book?" Tank asked as he played with a sugar packet from the little dish on the table. He knew how much those funny looking comic books meant to Keata. After all, he was in a foreign county with nothing familiar around except Kyoshi. Tank wanted to kill the men who had kidnapped the two. Although he was grateful to have Keata here, it was horrific what those traffickers had planned.

Keata sighed and shook his head. "I lay by bed. Now gone. Poof. No more." Keata flicked his fingers in the air to demonstrate disappearing into thin air. Tank thought the little guy comical.

"You'll find it. Try to remember last place you laid it down," Tank offered. Maybe someone wanted to read it and couldn't find him to ask. That would explain why it wasn't where Keata had left it, but it wouldn't explain *who* because it was written in Japanese.

"I try to, but no find. Someone maybe use?"

"Maybe. I'll ask around when we get home." Tank gave their choices when the waitress made her way over. Tank hated the way people gaped at him when he ordered his meal. He ordered three plates of fried chicken and mashed potatoes. He was a big guy and required a lot of calories. Keata sat there with his mouth hanging open. He liked the little man, but times like these made him uncomfortable.

"Sorry, Keata, but I have to use the restroom, and since I can't leave you out here alone you have to tag along." Tank slid from the booth. He chuckled when Keata just blinked up at him. Sometimes using short, broken words were difficult, and this was one of those times. He held his hand out, and Keata took it. Showing him would be easier.

When Keata saw that they were heading to the men's room he pulled at Tank's hand. "I sit by self. I grown man."

"Not now, Keata."

Keata pulled his hand free and crossed his hands over his chest, his lips pursed and his eyes rolled. Tank noticed his foot tapping as well. "Brat."

"Speak to hand." Keata threw his hand up.

"Fine. I won't hold your hand, but you *are* going to stand right inside the door.

"Fine." Keata threw his hands up and followed behind Tank.

Tank took care of business pretty quickly, washing his hands then drying them.

"See, that wasn't so hard."

Keata rolled his eyes once again and followed Tank back out.

By the time they made it back to their table, their food was waiting on them.

"Tank?" Keata stopped nibbling on his chicken strip. Tank looked up as the waitress brought his third plate over. They had to make room by shoving the sugar container and condiments aside, but all the plates fit.

"Yes, Keata?" Tank wiped his mouth with a napkin and stared down at his little friend.

He could see Keata struggling to find the words. It sucked that he wasn't fluent like his cousin, Kyoshi. Finally, Keata laid his hand on his stomach. "Cody, he make butterflies here." Keata lowered his head as if he were ashamed.

Tank's jaw dropped as his eyes widened. "You feel funny around him?"

"Yes. My belly tug to him. Why?" Keata implored, his eyes on Tank.

"You sad when Cody is gone?" Tank spoke in simple words, making sure he was fully understanding what Keata was trying to say. If he was interpreting him correctly, it answered the question a lot of the Sentries had been wondering. They knew one of the warriors was Keata's mate. They just didn't know which one, and neither Keata nor the guilty party volunteered that information.

"Yes, my heart always sad." Keata laid a hand over his heart, his small fingers clenching into his shirt. Tank could see the pain in the small man's eyes.

"I think he's your mate, Keata." Tank did not like this one bit. Cody was too busy running behind Jasper. Killer part was Jasper had a mate waiting on him—Zeus, the Alpha of the Eastern pack. It was a wonder they weren't at war because of Jasper's refusal to go to him.

"My boyfriend?" Keata looked at him confused.

"Yes."

"But he red-hair boyfriend." Keata looked even more confused now. How could Tank explain the complications of that screwed up relationship? He didn't even think an interpretation from his cousin Kyoshi would help this mess out.

Tank only half understood Cody and Jasper. Normally, he stayed out of it, but Keata now had a vested interest in it, and Tank wouldn't stand by to watch his buddy get hurt.

Tank was getting angrier by the moment. If Cody was indeed

Keata's mate, then this was one fucked-up situation, and Keata deserved better than Cody acting like an ass. Keata deserved someone who would love and cherish him. Tank almost wished Keata was *his* mate. There wasn't anything Tank wouldn't do for the little human.

For some reason fate decided it should be Cody, and Tank thought fate must have been drunk off of her ass when she decided to pair them.

"I don't know what to say, Keata." Tank fisted his hands. Cody had some damn explaining to do. "Finish eating, buddy."

His jaw clenched as he tried to eat. Keata sat there daintily as he ate. Cody was a damn fool. Tank dropped a tip on the table and had the rest of his meal tossed into a to-go container as he led Keata back out to his truck and took him home, forgetting about the post office.

Tank walked Keata into the house and headed straight for Cody's bedroom. He banged on the door, seething that Cody hadn't stepped up and claimed what was his instead of acting like a retarded wolf.

"What?" Cody barked as he swung his door open.

Tank shoved past him and stepped into the room. He turned and towered over Cody.

"I know you are aware of who Keata is to you. Why the fuck is he still unclaimed?" Tank wanted to throttle the wolf.

"That's none of your business." Cody had looked shocked for a moment then quickly recovered. Tank wondered if he was shocked that he knew or that Keata was his mate. No, Cody had to have known.

"It is my business when Keata is hurting. He feels the pull and can't understand it. He's sad when you aren't around, Cody. Figure your shit out, or I'll take Keata from you," Tank threatened.

"Try it," Cody snarled as he bumped chests with Tank.

"Why should you care? You're too busy with your head up your ass to even take care of your mate. Someone needs to." Tank stormed from Cody's bedroom to go find Keata. He had to make sure the little guy wasn't hurting. Had he known Keata was going through this, he would have stepped in a long time ago.

He found Keata sitting next to Loco, one of the other wolves that had been asked by Storm, Kyoshi's mate, to be Keata's sponsor. In other words, he was Keata's babysitter.

Loco was looking through a book as Keata laughed, and Tank's chest tightened at the unfairness thrust upon Keata. Cody was a damn fool.

"I find book!" Keata giggled excitedly.

Tank pulled Keata up and sat him on his lap, sitting next to Loco.

"Keata? Can I tell Loco about your belly?" Tank pushed a finger lightly into Keata's stomach.

Keata stared up at Tank then over to Loco, his expression hesitant. Tank thought Keata looked scared.

"What's wrong with his belly?" Loco's eyebrows knitted together.

Keata nodded at Tank.

"Nothing, except it gets all butterflies when a certain wolf is near him.

Loco's eyebrows shot up. "Who?" the warrior growled out menacingly. Tank knew how he felt.

"Cody." Tank rubbed Keata's back.

"Then why is he in your lap? It's forbidden to touch another mate intimately like that, especially a mate who hasn't been claimed yet," Loco stated disapprovingly.

"Apparently Cody doesn't want him, so the law doesn't apply." Tank shrugged.

"You've got to be fucking kidding? Who in their right mind wouldn't want Keata?" Loco looked over to the little man. "He is the most stunning man I've ever laid his eyes on. Cody has to be stupid. Blind. Loose screws. Something has to explain Cody's behavior."

"I'm thinking maybe we should give Keata that extra attention, and maybe, just maybe, a certain wolf will see the light and get his head out of his ass." Tank winked at Loco.

"You are a devious one. I think you're right." Loco had a gleam in his eye.

Tank nodded knowingly. Let Cody think his mate was going to be claimed by another. Let's see the Code-man stand down on this.

Chapter Two

Cody was torn. He knew Tank was right. He had been hoping Jasper would have gone to his mate by now. It wasn't that Cody had wanted to get rid of him, but he knew Jazz belonged to another, and Cody had come to terms with it.

He cared enough about his longtime friend not to claim his mate yet and flaunt it front of Jasper, but he was getting tired of waiting. Keata was his, and Cody had known that from the moment the little man had stepped through that door months ago. At first he was hesitant because Keata was so innocent, so fragile. He was confused as hell. Who wouldn't be? He wanted Keata, craved him.

"I am so fucked up in the head." Cody groaned aloud.

He jogged down the steps, seeking his mate. He found him in the den on Tank's lap. *Oh, hell no.* Tank had lost his ever loving mind.

This was the moment. Did he step up and claim what was his or continue to avoid it?

"I've been looking for you."

Cody turned to see Jasper standing behind him.

Just what he didn't need right now.

Why was Jasper always around when Keata was? It hurt his heart to see the two sharing friendship time together. He wanted to punch a wall. There was nothing he wouldn't do for his best friend, but he had to go to Zeus. It had hurt Cody when he first found out Zeus was Jasper's mate, but they both had known it would someday happen. He had to get this over with. He needed to explain to Jasper that Keata was his mate.

"I need to talk to you, Jazz. Come to my room." Cody cared

enough not to tell Jasper in front of everyone that he was claiming his mate and Jasper needed to do the same.

Cody led Jasper upstairs by his hand.

* * * *

Keata watched Cody take Jasper upstairs, and he knew they were going to kiss and touch. His heart felt like it was being ripped out of his chest. The tears fell as he laid his head on Tank's chest.

* * * *

Loco looked over in the direction of Keata's pain. What the fuck? Cody was actually leading Jasper upstairs to fuck him in plain view while his mate sat here to see?

Loco lost all respect for the wolf. He wanted to rip his throat out. Instead, he went for a run. If he confronted Cody right now, blood would spill.

* * * *

Cody sat Jasper on his bed.

"I need to tell you something. I'm not trying to hurt you, Jazz. Believe me." Cody paced back and forth in front of his bed. "Keata is my mate." There was no other way of putting it.

Jasper stared at him with his mouth hanging open. *"No way."*

"Yeah, I haven't claimed him yet because I didn't want to hurt you." He waited for the crying, the curses. He waited for Jasper's sarcastic personality to make an appearance.

He didn't expect the laughter.

"You're kidding? Oh, man." Jasper fell back onto Cody's bed, laughing.

"It's not funny, Jazz. Keata is suffering because of me. He feels the pull and doesn't understand it. I have to go to him." What the hell was wrong with Jasper? Cody clenched his jaw. Jasper was a jokester, but this wasn't the time for it.

"I'm laughing because the only reason I haven't gone to Zeus is because I was afraid of hurting you. Don't you see? We both have been afraid to claim what is ours because of the other. We were walking on eggshells, my friend." Jasper dried his eyes as he looked at Cody.

"Seriously?" Cody was shocked. Here he thought Jasper was mooning over him, fighting the pull to stay with him. He released a relieved breath.

"Yeah." Jasper sat up, his expression sobering. "Keata shouldn't be suffering. What the hell is wrong with you? Wait, my dumb ass is doing the same thing to Zeus. Scratch that. Truce?" Jasper held his hand out. Cody ignored it and pulled Jasper into his arms.

"Truce. We'll always be friends. If he does anything to hurt you, Jazz, I'll kill him." Cody hugged him tight then let him go.

"I'll miss you guys. It's scary, Cody." Jasper twisted his fingers in his lap. "It's a whole new pack. No den, no Cecil causing trouble or Johnny bouncing around. Hell, I'll even miss Oliver and his sour disposition."

"Oliver has mellowed since mating with Micah. We'll miss you, too. You can come hang out anytime you want. You know you're always welcome." Cody squeezed his hand. "Now go claim that mountainous man."

"He is huge, isn't he? He's hot, too." Jasper giggled.

"I don't know about hot, but I would say you made out pretty well."

"You did, too. Keata is beautiful. Treat him right, or I'll kick your ass. He's my buddy," Jasper teased.

They stood for a moment in silence then hugged one more time. "Gonna miss you most of all, Code-man."

"Same here, Jazz. Call me. Maybe we can go out to dinner some time. With our mates, of course." Cody opened his bedroom door as he and Jasper left his room.

"Sure. I'm gonna go pack and let Zeus know I'm coming." Jasper smiled.

"Love ya." Cody kissed Jasper on the cheek then ran to find Keata.

"You, too, Code-man." Jasper hurried to his room to make the arrangements.

* * * *

Johnny and Keata snuck into the kitchen, opened the refrigerator, and grabbed the ketchup. Keata hurriedly gave Johnny the Tabasco sauce.

"How much?" Johnny asked.

"I not know." Keata shrugged. "Whole bottle?"

"Sounds good to me." Johnny dumped the whole bottle of Tabasco sauce into the ketchup container and then replaced the lid, shaking it vigorously.

Keata ran over to the trash can and threw the empty bottle of Tabasco sauce away. "Hurry, someone come." Keata whispered.

Johnny threw the bottle back into the refrigerator.

They both ran over to the table and took a seat, pretending to sit there and talk.

Remi came in, heating up a plate of leftovers and grabbing the ketchup. Keata curled his lips in and looked over at Johnny, trying his best to hold back the snicker.

"What are you two into?" Remi asked as he pulled the plate out of the microwave.

"Not much, just hanging out," Johnny answered.

They both sat there watching as Remi dumped ketchup onto the food and then set the bottle down.

He took a bite and chewed, watching them watch him. Keata's

mouth dropped open as Remi turned a funny shade of red and then spit the food onto the floor, running around the kitchen, and waving his hands at his mouth.

"You think we do too much?" Keata asked Johnny.

Johnny was falling over in his seat laughing, Keata began to giggle at him, and then it turned into a full belly laugh.

"I'm gonna get you two." Remi snarled as he finished drinking the gallon of milk he was chugging.

"Run!" Keata and Johnny shot out of the kitchen, Remi close behind.

* * * *

Keata and Tank had gone down to the recreation center. "This is a place that helps the people here in town. Mostly kids come here and are poor, needing a place to safely play," Tank explained to Keata, who only understood a portion of what he was saying.

Tank was the little ones' favorite jungle gym. Keata stared in amazement as the little kids jumped all over the big wolf. The warrior just laughed and gave them all a ride on his shoulders. Keata would be frightened to be that high in the air. Tank was almost as tall as the Alpha. Tank had lifted him once to make a basket, but it wasn't that high.

Not knowing what to do, he reached down and picked up an orange ball. He remembered the game he had played with Oliver and Johnny. They had tried to make as many baskets as possible to win against the other mates who tried to beat them. The other team won, but Keata had had a lot of fun running around playing.

"This nice." Keata threw the basketball toward the hoop, missing for the umpteenth time. The thing was just too high up for him. He pouted when he missed once again. "You go in, or I be mad." He pouted and pointed at the ball.

It would be nice to make another one. He had made one when

they played the other team only because Tank had lifted him in the air for it. Oliver had tried to teach him how to make what he called a jump shot, but Keata seemed to be too short.

"Here you go, buddy."

"Whoa." Keata felt the same way he did the first time Tank had lifted him in the air. Like his stomach was falling out.

Tank laughed and lifted Keata up so he could finally make the basket. He laughed with joy when the ball rimmed it then fell through. His second shot ever. "Bull's-eye!" Keata shouted.

"She's pretty." One of the little girls stared wide-eyed at Keata.

Tank lowered Keata to his feet. He knelt down to seem less imposing. "That's a man, not a girl."

Keata felt his face heat at the little girl's mistake. It wasn't the first time.

"Oh, I'm sorry." She blushed and hid her face. Tank chuckled.

"No big deal. You wanna shoot some hoops?"

The little girl's head nodded rapidly.

Keata made his way over to the craft table. He watched the little kids bead necklaces. Following their lead, he picked the string up and lined brown and black beads up, placing a red heart between each color. He looked down at his work and noticed that the colors reminded him of his and Cody's eye colors.

"Not here, too." He groaned.

A tear welled up and ran down his cheek. Keata wiped it away as he grabbed the next color. The other mates didn't have to share, and Keata didn't want to either. If Cody was supposed to be his boyfriend, then why did the wolf ignore him and kiss and touch on the redhead wolf? The image of Cody taking Jasper upstairs still haunted him. Why didn't Cody like him?

"Don't cry." The same little girl had come over and hugged Keata around his waist. Keata smiled and hugged her back. He wiped another tear that had escaped.

"I not cry." He smiled as the little girl sat next to him and handed him the next color.

"I didn't mean to call you a girl. You're just so pretty." She looked up at Keata with big puppy dog eyes. How could Keata ever be mad at her?

"Not you. I have broken heart." Keata laid his hand over his heart then picked up his next bead that the little girl slid to him. Keata's stomach hurt with wanting Cody. Why couldn't Cody kiss and touch him? He would let him, although the thought was scary. He would. But Cody didn't want him, and he wasn't going to let the wolf as long as he still petted someone else .

"You okay, buddy?" Tank knelt down next to Keata.

"I okay." Keata smiled up at Tank. Even though he was kneeling, he was still taller than Keata. He was thankful for his big friend. He helped Keata understand what was happening and also had always been there for him.

Tank ran his hand over Keata's hair as he stood and wandered back over to the basketball hoops.

Keata took a deep breath and let it out. "No cry over spilt cow milk," he muttered.

He needed to cheer up. Keata had a cousin who loved him dearly and friends that took care of him. He had more than most people. So what if he didn't have the love of a man he would do anything for? He could live without it. Keata had to because Cody didn't want him. Although the thought was painful, he had to keep reminding himself of that fact.

"You ready, little one?" Tank approached the table after about an hour. Keata held his finger up to ask Tank to wait. He placed the last bead on the other necklace he had been working on. It had pretty pink and white beads in the shape of hearts. He laced it around the little girl's neck and smiled.

"Friends." Keata patted her hand then nodded to Tank.

* * * *

Keata ran excitedly through the door. He had made sparkly necklaces for all the mates and wanted to give them to each of his friends. His feet skidded to a halt upstairs when Cody came out of his room. Keata wondered if Jasper was in there. He tilted his head but couldn't see past the large wolf.

"Keata, wait." Cody held his hand up as he took a step forward.

Keata took a step back. He shook his head.

"Please. Can we talk?" Cody took another step only to have Keata take two back.

"We no talk. You love Jasper." A sob tore from Keata as he spun on his heels, ran to his room, and locked his door. He tossed the necklaces onto his dressers as he fell across his bed crying.

It hurt.

He didn't like this feeling. He didn't want to be a mate if it was this painful. A soft knock sounded on his door, but Keata ignored it. He didn't want to talk to anyone. A shroud of sadness surrounded him in a fog. He didn't want to leave his room ever again. It hurt too much.

After a moment the knocking stopped, and Keata rolled onto his side, holding his stomach to try and stop the pain. He eventually cried himself to sleep.

* * * *

Keata woke to someone knocking again, but this time the knocking was louder. He still ignored it until he heard Kyoshi calling his name from the other side. He didn't want to talk to Kyoshi.

He wanted to be left alone.

Kyoshi finally gave up and left him alone. Keata pulled one of his books from his dresser drawer and lay there reading the story. It was a love story.

Great. "It figure," he grumbled.

He tossed the book aside and grabbed the next one. Keata read into the night, ignoring his grumbling stomach. He would have to leave his room in order to eat, and he didn't want to see anyone.

"Keata, please," Cody called from the other side of the door. Keata looked over at his digital clock. It was two in the morning. What did Cody want? Why wasn't he kissing and touching Jasper? Maybe he wanted Keata to kiss both of them? Keata panicked at the thought. "No way." He scrambled to get under his blanket, hiding himself under there.

He was a virgin, and he wasn't throwing it away on someone that just wanted to play with him. No. Kyoshi drilled it into his head that he had to wait for that someone special and that once he gave it away there was no way to get it back, so Keata held onto it with a tight grip.

"Please," Cody begged again.

Keata glared at the door. He was tired of these feelings. He wanted to go out there and punch Cody in his arm. How dare he make him feel this way!

He stood, walking to the door and then chickening out at the last second and walked back over to his bed. He crossed his arms over his chest and tapped his foot, angry as heck.

Keata screwed his face up in irritation and then stormed back to the closed door, pointing at it angrily. "No way," he whispered, his lips twisting up in annoyance.

He paced in a circle, walking back over to the door and changing his mind about opening it a hundred times. "I not you toy," he whispered at the door again. "You not get this if you not want it." He pointed to his heart.

Keata walked over to his bed and picked his favorite manga up, throwing it at the bathroom door. "I not a toy!" This time he whispered a little louder.

He wasn't sharing himself, and that was final.

He crawled onto the bed and pulled the pillow over his head, drowning out the sound of the man he loved.

It still hurt too much.

* * * *

Cody wasn't going to give up. He knew he fucked up big time, and he knew groveling was in his future. A lot of groveling. He would do whatever it took to win his mate's trust. Loco had chewed him a new ass and also told Cody that Keata had cried when he saw Cody taking Jazz upstairs.

Cody had defended himself, telling Loco adamantly that all they did was talk and settle things between them. Loco calmed down somewhat after that.

He didn't care what the other warriors thought of him. All he wanted was Keata. His baby was hurting, and Cody desperately wanted to soothe him. That was impossible if he couldn't even get near his mate.

Cody knocked again, heard the soft cries, and his heart broke. He would leave Keata alone for now, but if his mate didn't come out in the morning, he was breaking the damn door down.

He slid down the wall and placed his back against Keata's bedroom door. Cody wasn't going to miss the opportunity to talk to his mate if Keata came out. He also felt a need to protect what was his, so he stayed by the door. *A day late and a dollar short, don't you think?*

God, I'm such a fucking idiot." He banged his head back.

Cody may have foolishly waited to claim his mate, but he was never far from Keata. He hovered when the little guy didn't know he was even around, and watched to make sure his mate was happy. It tore him up to see Loco and Tank take care of him. He knew the warriors wouldn't make any moves on him, but that didn't stop the urge to rip their throats out.

He cursed his stupidity. All his life he dreamed of his mate. Even when fooling around with his best friend, part of him craved it. When

Keata showed up, Cody's lack of common sense prevailed, his brain died, and he got stuck on stupid for months. It seemed no matter what his choice was, it hadn't been the right one.

"Sucks, doesn't it?"

Cody looked up to see Remi standing there. He nodded then stared down the hall in the opposite direction. He knew he fucked up. He didn't need anyone rubbing it in.

"You know you have to give him time. He's hurting because of your bad decision to wait. You should have been honest with him from the beginning." Remi sat down next to him. "Patience, my friend."

"Since when do you care how I feel?" Cody bit out.

"Always. Just because we toss barbs at each other doesn't mean I don't care. I'm not the big asshole you think I am." Remi chuckled.

Cody looked over at the wolf. He never really considered Remi a friend. They had always gone at it because of Jasper. Remi was always saying something insulting to his redheaded friend, and Cody had taken it personally. Now the guy was sitting here trying to support him?

"Yeah, I fucked up. I just wish he would talk to me." Cody banged his head back against the door again, frustrated and tired.

"Does he know Jazz is gone?"

"No. Do you think he thinks I'm still with Jasper?" Cody hadn't thought of that. He hadn't touched Jasper since Keata had walked into his life, but he knew the mates had filled him in on their love affair. Nothing stayed a secret in this place. Although he and Jasper were open about their relationship, it sucked that the mates informed Keata. Things would probably have gone a lot smoother it they hadn't.

"I would if I was him. He doesn't fully understand the whole mating thing, according to Kyoshi. Tread carefully with him, Cody. He's innocent, naïve." Remi stood and patted Cody on his shoulder.

God, this was messed up. His mate thought he was still fooling around with Jazz. He had to make him understand that they had parted as friends, not lovers. Cody needed to talk to his mate. Keata needed to know that he would never in a million years cheat on him. Although he loved Jazz as a good friend, now his mate held his heart.

"Keata," Cody begged through the door, "please. Jazz is gone. I don't want him. I want you, my mate."

Nothing. Why had he been such a fool?

Cody closed his eyes. *Please let Keata forgive me.*

Chapter Three

Keata listened to Cody begging. He didn't know what to believe. Jasper was gone? Did Cody only want him because Jasper was no longer here? His head hurt from trying to figure all this out.

Keata slid off the bed and padded across the room. He placed his hand on the door. "Leap of faith," he whispered. "'Cause you hurt heart, I beat with book." Keata waved his fist at the door.

Taking a deep breath, he unlocked the door and stood back. He prayed he wasn't making a big mistake. He knew he trusted too easily.

The door slowly opened, and Cody stepped in, closing it behind him. He leaned against the door, his eyes down. Keata stood there, tense. He wasn't sure what to expect.

Part of him was excited at the fact that Cody was here, and part of him wanted to kick him back out.

"I'm sorry, Keata. I was stupid. I didn't mean to hurt you." Cody shifted to his other foot, his head still hanging.

Keata had no clue what to say. He understood Cody's words. He just didn't know how to respond. What was Cody talking about? Why was he stupid?

"I not understand." Keata took a step back when Cody pushed away from the door he had been leaning against. His eyes were filled with anguish which made Keata wanted to reach out, but the wolf had always run from him when he tried. He wasn't going to be rejected again. Keata Kia was done being stupid for people. His needs had to start coming first because that was the only way he was going to be able to protect his heart.

"You're my mate. I…I wait to claim you. Jasper hurt, so I wait. I love Jasper—"

"No," Keata cried as he ran to the bathroom and slammed the door. He knew he should have kicked him back out. Stupid, stupid, stupid him. When was he ever going to learn?

"Keata, wait. Listen." Keata didn't listen as Cody shouted to him to wait. He leaned his head against the bathroom door, the pain unbearable. His hands clamped over his ears, unable to take the pain in Cody's voice.

So it was true. Cody was supposed to be his boyfriend, according to Tank, but the wolf just confessed to loving Jasper. His chest hurt with the grief he felt inside. His fists pounded the wall, angry at the way things were in his life.

"I love Jasper as friend, not boyfriend. I want you for boyfriend," Cody called through the door.

"No. You no want me," Keata cried from the other side. He slid down the wall and hugged his belly, the pain trying to come out. "You no want me," he repeated softly to himself.

"Fuck this." Keata heard the wolf shout as Cody snapped the handle and pushed the door open. He pulled Keata into his arms, but Keata fought him. If Cody thought he was just going to fall into his arms and forgive him, he had another thing coming.

Cody just stood there and held Keata as he pummeled his fists against Cody's chest. He finally exhausted himself and settled down as the tears started to come. No matter how much he fought to keep them in, they flowed like a broken dam.

The wolf carried him to the bed and sat down. Keata was held for what seemed like forever as he cried himself dry. Cody petted his back to try and sooth him.

"Feel better?" Cody asked when Keata hiccupped.

"No, heartbroken." Keata wiped his face as he tried to get out of Cody's arms. It felt too good, and that was bad. He didn't want to get used to being held only to have Cody run away again.

"Baby, I'm not going anywhere. Promise."

Keata's eyes widened when he realized he voiced his thoughts instead of thinking them. He hid his face in his hands, humiliated. His brain always seemed to melt around this wolf.

Cody chuckled. "I understood some of it, enough to know your fears now." Cody kissed his temple. "Look at me, baby." Cody pried Keata's hands away from his face.

"No, red-faced." Keata held his hands tighter to his face.

"Huh, do you mean embarrassed?" Cody leaned back to look down at him as Keata peeked through his fingers.

"Yes." Keata nodded and closed his hands back together.

"Don't be. Never be embarrassed with me." The wolf hugged him closer. Keata shouldn't be happy just to be held. The smell coming from Cody was good. He felt warm and tingly in the man's arms.

"Never?" Keata spread his fingers apart again and peered at Cody between them.

"No, never." Cody smiled a lopsided smile, and Keata's heart melted. He tried not to let Cody into his heart. Too late. But that didn't mean he had to give in so easily.

"You not want me," he said angrily, refusing to let that smile sway him.

"Yes, I did, I do. Jasper my best friend for long time. I didn't want to hurt him."

Keata stuck his bottom lip out. "So you act like I not here?"

"I fucked up. I'm sorry."

"Why I say okay?"

"Because I'm begging?" Cody grinned, and Keata almost gave in, almost.

"No, not good." He pointed his finger up at Cody. "You hurt again, and I not talk to you for long time."

"I don't plan on hurting you."

"We see." Keata twisted his lips and looked over at the bathroom, refusing to give in, and he would if he kept looking at the handsome wolf.

"You don't believe me?" Cody asked, gently tugging his chin back.

Keata narrowed his eyes. "I not so stupid as people think. I have feelings, and they hurt, too."

"Will you give me chance?" Cody pleaded.

Keata could see the fear and hope in the wolf's eyes.

"No hurt," Keata whispered to Cody. He couldn't take it if Cody hurt him again. He never wanted to experience that kind of pain again.

"Promise. No hurt," The wolf kissed the side of Keata's neck, his hand running down his back as he cupped Keata's butt.

Keata pushed at Cody's chest, shaking his head. "No earn." His lips thinned as he poked his finger into Cody's chest.

* * * *

Cody threw his head back and laughed. So he had to earn his mate's cock? No problem. He could do that. After what he had done, he would crawl through broken glass if Keata requested he do so.

"Then let's go eat." Cody stood with Keata in his arms, and his heart was lighter, taking him down to the kitchen. He knew his mate had skipped dinner, and Cody wasn't going to have him want for anything.

He sat Keata in one of the chairs and pulled out the chicken strips from the freezer. Cody had learned that Keata loved them. He wasn't the best cook in the world—he actually sucked at it—but he could fry them.

Cody moved around the kitchen, aware Keata watched his every move. Yeah, he showed off his prowess a little. He flexed more than he should have and hitched his hip to the side, seeing Keata staring at his ass. Cody reached up into the cupboard and flexed his biceps, smiling when he heard Keata's breath hitch.

"Here you go, babe." Cody placed the plate in front of him. He sat down next to his mate and cut his strips up, feeding them to him.

"I not a baby." Keata pouted.

Cody smiled, looking Keata up and down. "No baby, for sure." He growled softly as he leaned in to kiss Keata.

Keata pouted at Cody as he leaned back and stuck his hand up to stop him. "No. I say no earn."

"Okay." Cody relented. "Can I kiss you at least?"

Keata eyed him warily. "You try to trick me?"

"Promise, I'm not." Cody crossed his heart.

Keata nodded. "Only kiss. I watch sneaky hands," he warned.

Cody pulled Keata into his arms, cupping his face. Cody hesitated. He didn't want to rush this knowing his mate was innocent. Would this be his first kiss?

"Keata, have you kissed before?"

"No." Keata blushed as he leaned is head back and puckered his lips. Cody's heart swelled. He was just too damn adorable. He leaned forward as he lightly traced his tongue across Keata's puckered mouth.

Keata gasped.

"You like?" Cody felt his mate shake. His cock jerked, and Cody had to remind himself that Keata was only allowing a kiss.

Down, boy.

"Uh-huh." Keata's eyes were still closed, his head tilted back.

Cody could devour him. He was too damn pretty, lickable, suckable, and edible.

Keata held his hands in front of him, almost fisted in a prayer. Cody watched as Keata slowly opened his eyes.

"More?" he breathed in a hushed whisper.

Cody ran his hand down Keata's neck, laying a soft kiss to his lips, hovering close to feel Keata's warm breath caress him.

"More?" Keata asked again.

Cody smiled then ran his tongue across Keata's teeth. When Keata gasped, Cody thrust his tongue in, exploring Keata's sweetness.

"What the hell is going on in here, Keata?"

Cody growled as his arms wrapped around his little man.

"Don't growl at my mate, Cody," Storm warned him.

"Then tell him not to yell at mine," Cody snapped.

Storm and Kyoshi stood there with shock written all over their faces.

"You? You're his mate?" Kyoshi's expression turned from shock to anger, his face twisting up menacingly. "I thought you were fucking Jasper," he hissed.

Cody stood so fast the chair clamored to the floor. "I haven't touched Jazz since Keata walked through the front door."

"Let him go!" Kyoshi stepped forward, but Storm grabbed his arm, pulling him back.

"No, dragonfly. It is forbidden to come between mates." Storm looked down at his mate sadly.

"No, Keata. Don't," Kyoshi begged.

Keata clung to Cody. "Stormy eyes, take Kyoshi," Keata pleaded.

"If you hurt him, I will personally become your worst nightmare, Cody." Storm's face filled with angry promise.

Cody was pissed but knew they had a right to be angry. He had waited too many months, dodged Keata at every turn. All he could do was prove to everyone his intentions were true. He loved Keata, loved him the moment he laid eyes on him. Now all he had to do was convince Keata, and the rest would fall into place.

Cody inclined his head. "Never. I was a fool once. Never again."

Storm nodded, but his eyes told Cody that he would be watching him.

Cody grabbed Keata's plate then walked out of the kitchen with his mate still clinging to the front of him. He took Keata to his room, set the plate down on the dresser, and sat in the window seat. He wasn't ready to let his mate go just yet, so he held him in his arms.

"More?" Keata pushed up from Cody's chest, puckering his lips.

Cody was amazed Keata still wanted to kiss after the explosion in the kitchen. He ran his fingers through the satin hair, relishing the softness. Cody pulled Keata up to sit straight.

"You kiss me?" Cody wanted Keata to have a little more confidence with touching and exploring him.

Keata pulled Cody's head toward him, running his tongue across Cody's lips, mimicking what Cody had done downstairs. Cody moaned as his eyes closed. He was going to have a lot of jack off sessions until Keata agreed to let him claim him. Having Keata kiss him was pure eroticism. He fought against his canines descending, the urge to claim his mate was getting stronger the longer he touched and kissed Keata.

"More?" Cody mimicked Keata's word.

Keata smiled and deepened the kiss, his tongue sweeping into Cody's mouth. Cody could feel Keata's erection, and that only made his throb harder in his jeans.

Breaking the kiss, Keata stared into his eyes. "I like." He smiled shyly.

"Good. I want more." Cody sipped at his lips as his hands ran up and down Keata's sides. If kissing was all he was allowed right now, he was going to become a master at it. His lips would be permanently attached to Keata's.

His mate pushed at Cody's chest, his eyes becoming frightened.

"What's wrong?" All they were doing was kissing. Cody wasn't pressuring him for anything more. His eyes scanned the room. They were still alone. He listened, but it was silent. So what had his mate so afraid?

"Nothing." Keata lowered his head, his face turning red.

Was Keata embarrassed about his erection? That was the only thing Cody could think of. Keata was trying to hide it by placing his hands on his lap.

"Don't. You're supposed to feel that way with me." Cody grabbed his wrists and pulled his hands away, kissing each one, and then laid them on his chest.

"I no understand." Keata turned his head to the side, glancing at the floor.

"You will," Cody promised, running the back of his hand down Keata's beautiful face.

* * * *

Keata skipped down the steps. He carried the necklaces in his hand that he had made for the mates. He hoped they liked them. Keata had worked hard on them and was excited to surprise the mates with his gifts.

Keata thought about Cody and the kissing they had done. Okay, so he gave in a little too easily. Who wouldn't with a man as handsome as his mate? The manly smell had driven him crazy, and Keata was now addicted to those soft lips.

That didn't mean Cody was out of the cat house yet. He had a lot of making up to do, and Keata would make sure Cody kissed him as a part of his punishment. He giggled at his silly thoughts.

He rounded the corner into the den when Kyoshi stopped him. "Has Cody claimed you?" Kyoshi pulled at Keata's collar to look for the bite wound he heard all mate's received when claimed

"Stop." Keata pushed his cousin's hand away.

In his native tongue, Kyoshi spoke angrily. *"What have you done with him, Keata?"*

"That is none of your business. We are mates, and it's intimate. You know better than to have me discuss such things with you," Keata shot back, irritated that Kyoshi wouldn't accept the fact that he was an adult and could make his own decisions.

"Did you kiss him? Did your penis get hard?" Kyoshi tugged on Keata's forearm.

Keata pulled away and lowered his head. Why was Kyoshi being so mean? What Cody did to him was none of Kyoshi's business.

"I thought so. Do you know what Cody is going to do with his hard penis?" Kyoshi jerked Keata's head up to make him look into his eyes.

Keata took a step back. Kyoshi shouldn't be saying these things to him. It was private. He had no clue what Kyoshi spoke of, but he shouldn't be talking about Cody that way.

Kyoshi's eyes softened. *"I'm not trying to be mean, Keata. I'm trying to let you know you're not ready."*

"It my business," Keata yelled at him angrily and then ran from the den. He fled to his room and dropped onto the carpet. Why couldn't Kyoshi be happy for him? It wasn't fair. Keata balled his hands into fists and pounded them on the floor, throwing the necklaces across the room.

Why couldn't he be a happy mate like everyone else? It seemed that the gods themselves were out to keep him and Cody apart.

* * * *

Tank messed with the riding mower, trying his best to figure out why it wasn't working. He hated the fact that he was the one to discover it sputtering and stalling.

Maverick's philosophy around here was "You find it, you fix it," and Tank had been the one to find it broken.

"Hey."

Tank looked up from the "Do it yourself" printout the Alpha had given him to see Cody walking his way. He was still pissed as hell at the wolf. "What?"

"Glad to see my popularity is still so strong around here," he teased.

"Not funny and I'm not in the mood right now to listen to you." He tossed the paper on the ground. How the hell were you supposed to fix something from an internet printout? The Alpha may have money to hire a repairman, but he hated for strangers to come around.

That made life hell for the non-mechanically inclined warrior like him.

"I just wanted to apologize to you."

Tank stood and shook his head. "I'm not the one you should be apologizing to," he groused.

"I'm working on it with Keata. We're talking now."

Tank walked around to the other side of the riding mower and stared at it. He had no clue what the fuck he was looking at. He kicked it. Worked for his computer when the thing was on the fritz.

"Uh, I don't think that will help." Cody stared at him curiously. "Unless you're trying to tear it apart."

Tank rounded on him, pointing his finger within inches of Cody's face. "Look, I don't appreciate you coming out here trying to joke with me after hurting the little guy. He's my buddy, and seeing him hurt makes me want to hurt you."

Cody threw his hands up. "Fair enough. I don't honestly have to explain myself to you about me and my mate." Cody shot back. "But I thought we were friends, so I wanted to clear the air. If you think you're too big to listen, then fuck it."

Tank took a deep breath. "I don't know all the details, and I don't want to. Just tell me Keata isn't going to hurt anymore."

"Never again."

Tank nodded. "Then I'll think about forgiving your ugly ass."

"In your dreams. I'm the hottest warrior here."

Tank laughed. "After me."

"I can live with that."

* * * *

Maverick watched the two wolves hash it out in the backyard from the kitchen door. He had known all along that Keata was Cody's mate but refused to interfere.

Life had to unfold the way it was supposed to, but it didn't make watching Keata go through what he had any easier.

He smiled at what lie ahead for the two. If Cody thought Keata was timid and meek, he had another thing coming. The little mate was a spitfire waiting to blossom and discover his own strength.

And Maverick couldn't wait to see Cody run behind him like a love struck pup.

Chapter Four

"Hey." Cody walked over to his mate then sat on the floor in front of him and crossed his legs. "You okay?"

"No." Keata shook his head.

"What's wrong?" Cody reached out, curling his knuckles under Keata's chin, making him look into his eyes.

"Kyoshi say...say..." Keata blushed then pointed to Cody's crotch.

It took a moment for it to sink in, but Cody got the gist of it. "What? Did he say something about my cock?"

Keata slapped a hand over his mouth and giggled then nodded.

Cody let out a low growl. His mate was too sexy for words. "Can't I say cock?"

Keata giggled again.

"Is cock a funny word?" Cody was enjoying the laughter coming from his mate. The sound was making his heart sing.

"Funny word." Keata fell back laughing.

Cody crawled over him, hovering. "Should I say penis? Prick? Shaft? Tallywacker?" He began to laugh with Keata. His mate's giggles were contagious.

"Funny words." Keata giggled some more then sobered, grabbing Cody's shoulders and pulling him down. "More?"

Cody swooped down and devoured Keata's lips, his mate tasting sweeter than the finest wine. He ground his cock into Keata's.

With a look of pure panic, Keata pushed at his shoulders, demanding Cody move away. Keata scooted back until he was up against the wall. His knees drew up as he wrapped his arms around his legs.

"What's wrong, Keata? No hurt, promise." Cody was still on all fours, his eyes pleading with his mate.

"Scared," Keata said so low that if Cody didn't have superior wolf hearing, he would have missed it.

"Come here, baby." Cody sat back on his legs, his arms stretched out for his mate.

Keata crawled over to Cody, and he wrapped him in his arms.

"I know you're scared. I promise, no hurt." He rubbed Keata's back.

With a deep breath, Keata pulled out of Cody's arms and stripped naked.

Cody sat there dumbstruck for a moment. He quickly recovered and shot to the bedroom door, closing and locking it. He stood there staring at his naked mate.

Holy shit, he was beautiful. While his face took on feminine features, his body was all man. His skin was smooth and flawless except for the scar of the attack on his thigh. He could see Keata shaking, his hands at his sides. Keata was hairless except for his eyebrows and the hair on his head.

And what an ethereal sight that was.

His eyes locked onto the tattoo on Keata's chest. He had heard the mates snuck off to get them. He had even heard them question what Keata had possibly gotten, and now he knew. Cody stared at his name inked over his mate's heart. So Keata *had* known they were mates. There was a red heart above his name with blood red tears falling from it. His eyes closed briefly. Keata must have been in a lot of pain from not being near him to have that symbol.

Cody took a step forward, and Keata balled his hands into fists, bracing his shoulders and staring into Cody's eyes. He could tell Keata was trying to be brave. Cody bridged the gap and cupped his little man's face, making his mate look up. "So beautiful."

Keata gulped and laid his palms against Cody's chest. "Scared," he whispered once more.

"I know." Cody lifted Keata in his arms and carried him to the bed, laying him on his back. He ran his hands over the flat chest, tracing his name above Keata's heart. "Mine," Cody said more to himself then glanced up at his mate in wonderment. He ran his hands down Keata's sides then wrapped his hand around the jutting cock. His mate jumped.

Cody looked up into Keata's shimmering black eyes then smiled. "No hurt." He then leaned down and swallowed Keata's cock.

Keata keened loudly as he grabbed Cody's hair, pulling as his head thrashed from side to side. His legs fell to the sides, lifted and wrapped around Cody's shoulders. They fell again and then pulled up to his chest.

Cody smiled around Keata's prick. His mate was lost in lust, not knowing what to do about it. He grabbed Keata's ankles and placed his feet on the bed, sucking him deeper as Keata screamed out and shot down his throat.

Cody looked up to see a tear run down the side of Keata's face. He pulled off of him and sat back. "What's wrong, Keata?" Cody tilted his head to the side. He had thought his mate enjoyed it.

"First one. So good," Keata confessed.

"No way, seriously?" Cody was stunned. That couldn't have been his first orgasm. Could it?

"Yes way." Keata laughed as he wiped his face. "Sorry, cry like baby." Keata covered his face with his arm

Cody reached up and pulled Keata's arm away. "Don't. No embarrass."

Keata got a wicked gleam in his eye. "More?" He giggled.

Cody threw his head back and laughed. "More, more, and many more."

He lay back between Keata's legs, running his tongue around Keata's small sac, lapping at each orb. Cody pushed Keata's thighs up and rimmed his puckered hole.

"Cody," Keata cried.

Cody leaned up to see seed lying on Keata's belly. Oh fuck, his mate was the hottest man on the planet. He climbed above him and swirled his finger through it, coating his digit then lowering it and pushing past Keata's ring of muscles.

Keata stiffened, and Cody stopped moving, he waited until he felt the muscle relax then pushed a little further in.

"Want you, Keata." He leaned down and licked the spent seed from Keata's stomach.

"More." Keata groaned, his hips hitched and impaled Cody's finger deeper.

Cody pushed a second finger in, crooking them around. He grazed Keata's sweet spot and watched the fireworks explode.

Keata damn near flew off of the bed. He yanked Cody's hair as he floundered around.

Cody grabbed his hips and pressed him back down, holding Keata firmly.

"More," Keata cried, his hips pushing against Cody's hand again. "Cody, please."

"I got you, Keata." Cody added a third as he ran his canines down Keata's neck. The urge to sink his teeth in was overwhelming, but he knew Keata wasn't ready for that. He needed to be buried inside his mate first.

Cody added a fourth finger, knowing Keata needed as much stretching as possible with his size.

"You okay?" Cody asked while sucking Keata's nipple into his mouth. His mate's skin was heady. Cody lapped at his chest, kissing the tattoo and promising himself to cleanse Keata of those blood red tears. He sucked in the other nipple, rolling it around in his mouth. It peaked to a small point. Cody bit gently at it and then kissed his way back to the other one.

"Yes," Keata hissed out, pressing his chest into Cody's mouth.

Cody reached for the lube in the nightstand and came up empty-handed. Crap, Keata didn't have any. Didn't his mate jack off?

Duh, that would be a no if the guy just had his first orgasm.

"Keata, no lube?" Cody's cock was throbbing to get inside his mate. It pressed against his zipper in a painful arousal.

Keata tilted his head and furrowed his brow. "I not understand."

"Never mind." *Think, dammit.* Cody shot off of the bed and ran to the bathroom. He riffled through Keata's medicine cabinet, knocking things into the sink until he found a jar of petroleum jelly. Fuck it when in a pinch.

Cody ripped his clothes off on his way from the bathroom, and then set the jar on the nightstand. He opened the lid, and then smeared the thick petroleum jelly around Keata's ass and his own cock, pushing his fingers back into Keata for good measure. Cody grabbed Keata's prick, stroking it a few times to get his mate to relax. This seemed to do the trick because Keata went from trembling to moaning.

Cody lined himself up with Keata's tight hole. His own body started to shake, the anticipation of finally mating Keata shot through him like a lightning bolt.

"Ready?" Cody slid his left hand under Keata's shoulder, staring at him deep in his midnight black eyes.

"Yes." Keata's body trembled again, and Cody knew there was no amount of stroking to settle his mate's nervousness

"I won't move until you tell me when I can." He never looked away from Keata as he slowly pressed in. Cody fought for control. His mate's tight star threatened his sanity as he inched in a little at a time.

His right hand slid under Keata's other shoulder, cradling his mate close to his chest. He was buried balls deep, and the need to move drove him insane, but he would never hurt his mate.

Cody rested his forehead on his man's chest, breathing in and out to stave off his orgasm. There was no way in fuck he was going to last long the first time. Months of need and want had come to a head, and he begged fate to let him last long enough to show Keata that sex was a beautiful thing between mates.

"More." Keata wiggled his ass, and Cody nearly unloaded right then and there. When his mate's small nails dug into his shoulders, Cody had to rapidly breathe in and out to stop his balls from emptying.

His hips rocked back and forth, moving his right hand down until it cupped Keata's ass as he pulled his mate's hips a little higher then slanted his head and took Keata's lips in a searing kiss. His left hand massaged the back of Keata's head, his fingers luxuriating in the silky strands.

Keata made the cutest little noises as Cody made love to him. He began to speak in his native tongue, his head falling back as his nails dug deeper into Cody's flesh. He would wear Keata's marks with pride.

"Cody." Keata pushed his hips higher, grinding his cock into Cody's stomach. The little hellcat wrapped his legs around Cody's waist and began fucking him back. Cody was surprised, and then he recovered quickly enough to drive deeper, harder, as Keata's mewling grew louder.

Watching his mate enjoy his touch was like watching the sunset from Heaven. He nuzzled into Keata's neck, sucking up his skin as Cody pulled back and then thrust in.

He stilled for a moment, allowing Keata the pleasure of riding him upside down. Keata moved up and down wildly and uncoordinated. The movements drove Cody closer to the edge.

Cody reached between them and grabbed Keata's shaft and squeezed the head, pre-cum leaking onto his fist. He used it for lube. He didn't have to pump his fist. All he had to do was hold Keata's cock, and his mate's fucking motion did the rest.

"Do you accept me as your mate, Keata?" Cody panted.

"Yes, Cody, yes," Keata shouted as he rode harder.

Cody sank his teeth into the soft flesh of Keata's shoulder. Keata wailed as his seed erupted into Cody's hand. His mate hitched his hips faster into Cody's fist, his hips jetting up and down. Cody growled around his mate's neck.

Cody closed his eyes as he felt his life ribbons unwind then entwine with Keata's. The feeling stealing his breath of joining with his mate. Their heart beats synchronizing, the mating complete. He pulled at Keata's neck, drinking down his ambrosia in frenzy. He couldn't seem to get deep enough into Keata to satisfy his hunger for his mate. The little guy was going to be his undoing, and he knew it.

Throwing his head back, Cody roared his release, pumping faster into Keata ass. He dropped his head and licked the wound closed, lapping the blood up that had escaped. Cody's mind fogged with the overwhelming love the encompassed him at having his mate in his arms.

"Mine," Cody crooned as he slowed his pace, rocking slowly and staring Keata in his eyes. His mate was the most beautiful creature on earth in his eyes. Cody felt his cock softening, so he pulled free. He wrapped his body around Keata's, not caring of the semen cooling between them. Removing it could wait, he only wanted to feel his mate's soft skin against his at the moment.

"Mine," Keata mimicked and then kissed Cody.

* * * *

Keata ran down the stairs and into the den the next morning.

"I claimed, I claimed," he shouted over and over again as he threw his hands in the air and ran around the pool table then the couches. He threw a sparkly, beaded necklace at each mate as he ran around every piece of furniture in the room.

"No way." Blair and Oliver jumped up to stop Keata. "Who?"

Cecil and Johnny tossed their controllers down and ran over to Keata as Drew came from behind the bar to join them.

"Cody." Keata beamed.

"But I thought—"

Blair shot Drew a warning look. Drew curled his lips in to hush anymore questions.

Oliver pulled Keata's collar back. He knew the mate would see the healing wound of teeth marks. Keata beamed at the fact he was now a mate. "Yep, he's been claimed."

"Well, this is a cause for celebration." Cecil clapped his hands together then rubbed them back and forth.

"What are we celebrating?" Kyoshi asked as he entered the den. He spotted Keata and lowered his head. "I'm sorry, Keata."

Keata pushed through the other mates and ran to Kyoshi, throwing his arms around his cousin's shoulders. "It okay."

Kyoshi hugged Keata tight. "So sorry."

"We are celebrating Cody claiming Keata," Cecil informed him.

Kyoshi leaned back and pulled Keata's collar aside.

Keata pulled away from Kyoshi. He didn't want another lecture from his cousin or more intimate questions he definitely wasn't going to answer. Last night had been magical, and he didn't want Kyoshi taking away from it.

Kyoshi pulled Keata back into his arms, whispering in his ear, "Did it hurt?"

Keata giggled and whispered back, "No. I like very much." Boy, did he ever. Keata wanted to run upstairs and do it all over again, but he was being hip with the men now and he couldn't be happier.

"Me, too." Kyoshi laughed.

"So, are we going to celebrate?" Cecil stepped closer to the pair.

"Yes, celebrate…what celebrate?" Keata turned to Kyoshi for an explanation.

"Go dancing," Cecil offered.

"Oh, I like dancing. Okay." Keata squealed when Johnny hugged him tightly from behind.

"We dance together, Keata." Johnny bounced him around.

Keata giggled and swatted at Johnny's hands. When the mate put him down, Keata and Johnny began to dance to imaginary music together.

"Where?" Drew asked.

Keata settled down and listened to the mates.

"I was thinking that new nightclub that just opened up by the mall." Cecil waited for their responses.

"Will we have to steal one of the cars?" Blair asked with a devilish gleam in his eyes. Keata wondered what was going on and why Blair had that look.

"Possibly." Cecil clasped his hands behind his back and rocked back on his heels.

"Then I'm in." Blair rubbed his hands together. "When?" Oliver asked.

"We meet by the front door at ten p.m. and make sure your mates are otherwise occupied with something else." Cecil turned to Kyoshi, "Explain all that to Keata. We don't need him blabbing to Cody." Cecil tapped knuckles with all the mates then headed down the hall toward his mate's office.

"That is one sneaky dude." Kyoshi shook his head as he laughed.

"You've no idea." Blair snorted.

Keata was totally lost here. All he knew was they were going dancing, and he bubbled with excitement at the idea.

* * * *

Keata and Johnny crept into the den, looking around to make sure no one was around. Keata tried to hide the bulge under his shirt as the two made their way over to the video game controllers.

Keata lifted his shirt and pulled the bag out, handing it to Johnny as he looked over his shoulder.

"Hold the controller." Johnny handed it to him as he took the jar from the bag. They made quick work and then shoved the jar and bag under the couch and sat down.

Cecil and Oliver came into the den and turned the television on, starting the Xbox game. They jumped around playing as Keata and Johnny watched.

"Damn, it's hot in here." Oliver wiped his hand over his forehead.

"Dude, you got something on your face." Cecil pointed and then scratched his chin.

"You, too." Oliver pointed at Cecil's face. They both ran over to the mirror behind the bar and looked. They had black face paint all over their faces and hands.

They spun and glared at Keata and Johnny, who were laughing hysterically on the couch.

The two shot off the couch and down the hall, racing to Maverick's office. They ran through the door and straight behind Maverick's chair.

"What's going on?" Maverick turned to the two and asked.

Just then Cecil and Oliver came running into the room."You two." Cecil growled and pointed at them.

"What the fuck?" Maverick looked over at the painted pair.

"They smeared the controllers with face paint and waited for unsuspecting victims to use them," Oliver snapped.

"Go clean up. I'll have a talk with these two."

Keata watched Cecil and Oliver storm from the room. He gulped when the Alpha turned to them. Were they going to be punished?

A wide grin broke out across the wolf's face. "Good one." He held his hands out, palms up. "Give me five."

Keata watched Johnny slap Maverick's hand, so he did the same. "Don't let them catch you." He laughed.

Chapter Five

Cody's jaw tightened as he searched the Den for Keata. It wasn't like his mate to not be in his bedroom, the den, or the kitchen, his three favorite rooms. The wolf even checked the backyard, the other bedrooms, the front yard, and the dining room.

His anxiety grew by the minute when he didn't spot any of the other mate's around.

Cody was livid by the time he jogged into Maverick's office. "I can't find Keata anywhere, none of the mates, and one of the SUVs is missing."

Maverick's fist slammed down on his mahogany desk. "Dammit, Cecil. Did Gunnar install those GPS tracking devices like I asked?"

"Don't know, but I'm about to find out." Cody ran from the office and searched the rooms until he found Gunnar in the library. He would die if something happened to Keata. His mate was too trusting, too naïve. What if he trusted the wrong person and something happened to him? Shit, his heart was in his throat.

"Gunnar, did you get those GPS tracking devices installed?" Cody asked out of breath.

"Yeah, why?"

"Mates and one of the SUVs are gone."

"Dammit, Cecil." Gunnar tossed his book aside and pushed up from the couch. "Let's go."

* * * *

The mates chattered excitedly as Blair drove them to the club. He cranked the music up to get the party started as the mates chatted excitedly. Oliver and Cecil began dancing in their seats, bobbing their heads, and waving their arms in the air.

"This fun." Keata giggled from behind Blair. He smiled, glad to see Keata happy again. He snickered when he thought of what Oliver had told him about the little guys' prank. No harm, no foul. Cecil and Oliver agreed to let it go, for now.

Blair watched the city lights come into view, and his heart began to race. He loved where he lived now, but sometimes cabin fever threatened to choke the shit out of him.

He pulled into a parking spot next to the club and parked the SUV. Everyone buzzed louder with excitement as they climbed out.

Blair raised his hand to quiet them down. "Okay, everyone pair up. No one is to dance with anyone but another mate. Got it?" he instructed them.

"I want Keata." Johnny bounced on his heels, grabbing Keata's hand tight. Keata nodded his approval as he beamed up at Blair and held his and Johnny's hand up to show they were together.

"Okay. Cecil, you're with Drew and Oliver. I'll take Kyoshi." Once everyone gathered with who they were supposed to be with, they headed into the club.

The music was thumping, pop music drowning everything out as the mates pushed their way onto the dance floor. Blair couldn't believe how packed it was. He worried that the smaller mate's would get lost, so he pulled Kyoshi closer and kept an eye on the others.

He started dancing with Kyoshi as Oliver threw his hands up and let Drew and Cecil dance around him. It was good to see Oliver so happy.

"Aw hell, this is my song." Drew jumped around like he was being hit with resuscitation paddles shocking him back to life. His lips twisted in concentration, trying his best to look hard core.

Blair threw his head back and laughed as Keata and Johnny tried their best to sing along with Jeremiah. They were so off key and off lyric he was waiting for the artist to come into the club and snatch his club mix back.

"Dude, you have to hush them. It sounds like animals are dying in here." Cecil grinned from ear to ear.

"I hear you." Keata stuck his hand up to tell Cecil to speak to it. "Give dap." He held his fist up to Blair.

Blair's mouth hung open, but he gave it to Keata.

The guy mates and now he's corrupted? Or is his true sparkling personality coming through?

Blair bounced his shoulders, rocking back and forth, getting his groove on. Cecil moved in front of him, and the pair set the dance floor on fire.

It had been too long since Blair had this much fun. The club felt like a breathing entity as they danced their hearts out.

They stayed exceptionally close to Keata and Johnny, the smallest and most naïve of the mates, or so Blair thought.

Kyoshi was shorter than Johnny, but he was too smart to fall for anything anyone may try. Blair watched him dance and giggled to himself. Kyoshi tried his best to glide around and shake his booty.

After the second song, Keata and Johnny panted that they were thirsty. Blair and Kyoshi pushed through the throng of bodies as they made their way to the bar. Blair held his hand up until the bartender acknowledged him.

"Seven orange sodas please."

The bartender stared at him strangely. "You do know you're in a club?"

"Yeah, so?" Blair glared at him.

"Seven orange sodas it is." The bartender filled the glasses with ice then sprayed the orange soda into each glass.

Blair pulled his wallet out, but the guy raised his hand. "On the house." He winked at Blair.

Blair shoved his wallet back into his pocket then grabbed the glasses along with Kyoshi. He knew the guy was flirting, but Blair wouldn't fool around on Dakota in a million years. He thanked the man then pushed back through with drinks in hand.

Keata and Johnny drank their sodas down until they sucked air. "Thanks." Johnny handed his glass back to Blair as did Keata then they began to flounder around again. Blair arched an eyebrow at them. These two needed to get some rhythm in their lives.

"I can help with those."

Blair turned to see a slim man standing beside him. His hair was jet black and hung to his shoulders. His skin was pale and his eyes...glowing red. What the fuck? Blair took a step back, his instincts yelling at him to grab the mates and run like hell.

"I–I got it." He and Kyoshi took the empty glasses back to the bar and sat them down, rejoining the other mates once more. The guy was gone, but Blair still had an urge to get out of there.

They danced a few more songs, changing partners, and enjoyed the night. Keata threw his hands in the air and rocked his hips unsteadily from side to side, not matching the beat, as Johnny danced circles around him doing the robot. Blair laughed when they kept bumping into each other. Oliver was trying to dirty dance with Kyoshi, but the little mate kept punching Oliver in the gut when he got too close. Oliver laughed, and so did Blair.

Blair could have sworn Drew was doing some sort of body wave, or having a seizure, as Cecil danced his ass off. The Alpha's mate had some rhythm and moves to his little self.

Blair swayed his hips as he circled Oliver and then the brothers started dancing together.

The man with glowing eyes stepped back to Blair, trying to grab his hips and dance behind him.

"He's with me." Oliver stepped up and grabbed Blair from the stranger's clutches.

The stranger glared menacing at Oliver but stepped back.

"I think we need to go," Blair whispered into Oliver's ear. Oliver nodded. They gathered the rest of the mates, heading for the door when the stranger grabbed Blair by his wrist, stopping him from leaving.

"Let him go," Johnny shouted and smacked the guy's arm.

The stranger hissed, his fangs gleaming in the club lights.

"Oh shit," Blair yelled as he tried to yank his arm free. What the fuck was this dude?

The stranger pulled Blair into his arms as Blair struggled to get free.

"Let him go."

Blair suddenly fell to his ass as he looked up to see Dakota's hand wrapped around the stranger's throat. Three more fanged men had joined the stranger. Maverick, Hawk, and Cody stood in front of them, daring them to interfere.

Murdock, Tank, Gunnar, and Ludo tried to get the mates out, but five more fanged men crossed their arms over their chests and blocked the door.

The warriors pulled the mates into a tight formation, blocking them from the fanged men.

"Enough!"

Blair looked up to see a suave man saunter forward. He had on crisp slacks and a flowing black silk shirt. His raven dark hair stopped a little past his shoulders, and his eyes glowed like the rest of the men surrounding them.

"What is the meaning of this?" the suave stranger asked.

Blair pointed to the man who harassed him. "He won't leave me alone."

The suave stranger looked down to the man in question.

"I want him." The stranger hissed.

"He's my mate." Dakota clenched his hand tighter around the guy's throat.

"Ah, I was not aware there was a wolf pack in the area." The suave stranger stepped closer.

"And you are?" Maverick matched his steps, standing his full six nine height.

"I am Prince Christian, and this is my coven. I assume you are their Alpha?" Christian nodded toward the warriors.

"I am." Maverick nodded.

"Christo, you have an apology to make." Christian glared at the vampire that had tried to claim Blair.

"I did not know, Christian." The man bowed his head, or tried to, around Dakota's hand at his throat.

"You are?" Christian turned back to Maverick.

"I am Maverick Brac, Alpha of the Brac Pack." He extended his hand, and Christian shook it.

"Are there any more packs that I should be aware of?" Christian released Maverick's hand.

"Yes, the Eastern pack is run by Zeus."

"My apologies. My men were not aware of you. They will be now. On my honor you have my word that no mate shall be touched. Please, stay. Enjoy." Christian pulled Christo from Dakota and threw him toward the back of the bar. "He will be dealt with for encroaching on your mate." Christian inclined his head toward Dakota.

"Thank you." Maverick inclined his. "Our ancient scrolls tell us that you live in South America."

"We have expanded." Christian splayed his arms wide. "But no fear, your mates are safe."

* * * *

Cody pulled Keata to his side, his mind whirling at the idea that vampires existed.

"She is safe as well, wolf." Christian eyed Keata.

"He." Cody corrected him.

"Really? He is very beautiful." Christian looked at Keata a little more closely, making Cody's hairs rise.

"He's *my mate*," Cody clarified with a snarl.

"And he is safe as well, on my honor." Christian walked away with Maverick, deep in conversation. The other vampires moved away slowly, allowing the warriors to pull the mates from the club.

Keata shook in Cody's arms. "He no take me?" his mate asked as he clung to Cody.

"No one is taking you from me, Keata." Cody didn't trust the look Christian had given Keata. He was going to be sure Keata stayed by his side.

* * * *

"You have to be careful, Keata. You can't leave without telling me. I must know where you are at, at all times. Don't go anywhere else with the mates without telling me. Don't go anywhere with one of the warriors without telling me. I don't want you wandering outside either," Cody rambled on. Keata just blinked at him, trying his best to understand what Cody was saying.

"Ugh." Cody grabbed Keata's hand and pulled him from the room, walking down the hall and knocking on Storm's door.

Storm arched an eyebrow when he saw the frazzled look on Cody's face. "I need to talk to your mate."

The large warrior stepped aside and waved them in. Kyoshi was over by the dresser, putting clean laundry away.

He ran over to Keata and hugged him, speaking in his native tongue. *"I saw the way that nasty vampire was staring at you. You must go nowhere without your mate. Understand me, Keata? I don't want you running off with Cecil or anyone else, not even Tank or Loco. Okay?"*

"Okay. Are there really vampires?" Keata looked at Kyoshi with wide eyes.

"It appears so. Promise me, Keata. Nowhere without Cody." He squeezed Keata's forearms.

"I promise. They scare me." Keata gulped.

"Can you tell Keata not to go anywhere without me knowing, not even with other mates or warriors?" Cody ran his hand through his hair.

"Already did. He promised not to. You really love him, don't you?" Keata stared up at Cody.

"With every breath I take, Kyoshi. I would never let anything happen to him." Cody pulled Keata into his arms.

Kyoshi nodded. "Fair enough. I'll back off. I just love him so much."

"I know. He's in good hands." Cody thanked Kyoshi and Storm then took Keata to their room.

* * * *

"I have called this meeting of all Sentries and mates to make you aware, as I'm sure you are, that vampires have moved into the area. I knew they existed, but they were far enough south for so many centuries I didn't think them a problem." Maverick leaned back against the pool table. The mates sat on the warriors' laps while the unmated warriors stood behind the couches in the den.

"Do you trust Christian?" Tank asked.

"I don't know yet. He seems sincere, but that doesn't mean he doesn't have rogue vamps like we have rogue wolves. I never thought they would come this far north, but since they have, be on alert. I've called Zeus and warned him as well." Maverick turned to his mate, his eyes narrowing, "No more running off by yourself or with the other mates, we clear?"

"Yes." Cecil had only wanted to celebrate Keata's mating. He had no idea they would be in such danger. Maverick had chastised him last night, making Cecil feel a foot tall. Maverick had been gentle about it, but Cecil took it to heart. He only wanted the mates to have fun, not put them in harm's way.

"Do they really suck blood and do all the crap you see in the

movies?" Oliver twisted in Micah's lap as he looked toward Maverick.

"I don't really know and, to be honest, Oliver, I don't want to ever find out. I don't want any of you finding out either." Maverick stared at each of the mates in turn.

* * * *

"Are they real?" Jason asked Gunnar from behind the bar. He had called his Alpha Zeus to tell him about what was going on. While Zeus thanked him, he also reminded Jason that he was now Brac pack and needed to give his loyalties to Maverick.

Jason wondered why his *ex-alpha* had just traded him off like yesterday's underwear. Zeus told him that it was Maverick who had requested him. Why? He didn't even know the Alpha. Why would he want him?

"Yeah, seen it for myself."

Jason was shook from his thoughts at Gunnar's reply. He had forgotten he even asked a question.

"Do you think they'll come this way? The city is a pretty good distance from us." Not only did they have to fight rogue wolves, but now vampires?

"I hope not, things would get ugly around here. This Prince Christian swore our mates were safe, but he said nothing of us warriors or our Alpha." Gunnar ran his hand through his hair.

If they did come this way, how did one defeat someone who was already dead? They needed to find out more about these creatures. Knowledge was power. Jason wholeheartedly believed this.

Chapter Six

Cody snuck up on Keata, who was dancing around the den playing video games. He crouched down and slid around the couch, crawling out and grabbing his ankle.

"Ahhhh!" Keata screamed and jumped into the air, losing his balance. Cody caught him before he fell on his butt.

"No nice, Cody!" Keata yelled at him as he clutched his chest.

Cody laughed his ass off as he dropped to the couch with Keata, kissing his mate until he settled down.

"No nice, but fun." He wrapped his arms around Keata and laid his forehead against his little man's. "Love you." Cody kissed Keata's lips in a quick peck.

"Really? Cody love me?"

"Really." Why did Keata look so shocked?

"Keata love Cody, too." Cody chuckled when Keata squealed an unmanly sound as Cody tossed him over his shoulder and jogged upstairs, taking the steps two at a time.

He deposited his mate on the bed, crawling over him like a predator. Keata giggled and scooted away, running from Cody.

"If you run, I chase," Cody warned.

"No catch," Keata teased as he shot out of the bedroom door, peals of laughter trailing behind him as Cody gave him a moment to get a head start. He could catch his mate easily, but he wanted Keata to have fun with it.

Cody hopped off of their bed and began his hunt. He knew Keata was close because he could feel his mate's excitement pouring off of him. He passed a door and heard giggles trying to be suppressed. He smiled and passed the door up, allowing his mate to continue the game just a little longer. Keata shot out of the room as soon as Cody had passed it and ran in the opposite direction.

Cody pressed the palm of his hand into his erection. The thrill of the chase was a fucking turn on. "Gonna find you, mate," Cody warned as he turned down another hallway and saw Keata's little toes sticking out from behind the heavy drapes covering a window. Cody bit the inside of his mouth to stop the laughter as he got down on his hands and knees and crawled toward the wiggling toes. Keata was tee-heeing quietly.

"Gotcha." He snagged his mate by his legs and pulled him forward. Keata erupted in snorts and giggles as Cody pulled him into his arms.

"Cody no fair. Wolf help." Keata pouted as he wrapped his arms around Cody's shoulders.

"My wolf didn't help. You noisy." He carried his precious package back to their bedroom, this time locking the door. His mate wasn't escaping again. Cody pulled Keata free of his clothes and tossed him on the bed gently as he stripped out of his.

"Wow." Keata stared between Cody's thighs, his eyes huge.

"You like?" Cody flexed and posed for his mate, proud Keata approved of him.

"Really like." Keata licked his lips, and Cody's cock jumped at the chance to be licked like a lollipop. He knew Keata had never done it before, but he would gladly take whatever Keata could manage.

"Wanna taste?" He grabbed his cock in his hand and waved Keata to the edge of their bed.

"I–I…" Keata looked intimidated by the request, his eyes shooting from Cody's cock to his eyes.

"I know. I'll teach you." Fuck if this wasn't a huge turn-on. He was Keata's first in everything, and Cody couldn't have been more pleased with that.

"Okay." Keata crawled over and sat back on his knees. "How?"

"Stick your tongue out." Pre-cum dripped from Cody with the anticipation building like static electricity. He prayed he made it through the lesson without premature eruption. Keata was everything he ever wanted and more.

Keata stuck his tongue out as he laid his hands on Cody's muscular thighs. Cody rubbed the head of his cock across Keata's tongue, and a moan ripped from his chest.

"Yes," Cody hissed, "suck it, Keata."

Keata closed his lips around the bulbous head, and Cody fought to stave off his impending orgasm. This was too much.

His mate sucked and licked, slob dripping down his chin as he drew the clear liquid from Cody's cock. Damn, his mate was a fast learner. Cody reached down and grabbed one of Keata's hands and placed it on his balls, rolling Keata's hand around then gently squeezing them, never letting his mate's hand go.

"So good, Keata." Cody's head fell back. He began to move his hips slightly, not being able to stop them.

He gasped when Keata took him deeper into his throat, moving his head up and down. Cody's nerve endings came to life and ricocheted off of one another. If he didn't stop Keata, he would shoot into his mouth, and he knew his mate wasn't ready to take his load yet.

"Lay on your back."

Keata looked up at him from under his thick black lashes while his lips were wrapped around Cody's cock.

Cody lost it at the erotic sight, and semen shot from his cock before he could pull away. He shouted out Keata's name as wave after wave of seed was pulled from his balls.

He yanked his hips back, dropping to his knees and kissing Keata as though his mate carried the breath of life for him.

"You like?" Keata asked with a wicked grin on his face as he wiped Cody's seed from his chin. Cody grabbed his hand and licked the spent sperm from his fingers.

"Love," he cooed as he laid Keata onto his back, reaching into the drawer for the bottle of lube. "I make love to you, Keata."

"Yes, please." Keata pulled his knees to his chest, looking at Cody in such awe that Cody had to pull his eyes away. There was nothing in this world he wouldn't do for Keata. No battle he wouldn't fight for him, no request he wouldn't fulfill. His soul belonged to his five-foot-two mate forever.

Cody slid a wet finger into Keata, caressing his soft skin with the other hand. His cock had come back fully to life at the prospect of being inside him.

"More."

"God, I love that word." Cody slid another finger into his mate, scissoring them apart. He could feel the love radiating from Keata. He slipped a third finger in, pushing it back and forth and watching the bliss cross Keata's face.

"More." Keata panted, fisting his hands in the sheets. His head tilted back and a groan left his lips.

Cody pulled free and lubed his cock for its journey home. He hitched Keata's small rounded butt up then pushed in, his breath catching at the tightness sliding down his cock as he seated himself.

"Oh god, Keata. Feels so damn good." Cody fell to his arms, keeping the weight there and away from his small mate.

"So good." Keata moaned as he started to move. He cupped Cody's face and pulled him down for a kiss as he wrapped his legs around Cody's waist. "Love me, Cody," he whispered across Cody's lips.

"Forever." Cody began to thrust into his mate's tight, puckered hole, his love deepening further for Keata. His canines dropped, his eyes glowing as he thrust deeply.

"My wolf. Bite me." Keata tilted his neck to the side, arching his back giving Cody room for a deeper penetration.

Cody sank his teeth in as he rocketed into Keata, cries and mewls at his ear from Keata's lips.

Hot wetness splashed Cody's abdomen, and he knew his mate had come. He drank deeper as the ring of muscles clamped down around his cock, making it almost impossible for Cody to move as Keata's ass locked his cock into place. He waited for it to relax before he thrust harder, deeper. Cody licked his neck and screamed into Keata's neck as he bathed Keata's channel with his seed.

"Keata, Keata, Keata," Cody chanted repeatedly into his mate's neck, never tiring of that beautiful name.

"My Cody." Keata petted his hair.

Cody fell apart in his arms. His tears ran down his mate's neck as a sob tore from him. Keata wrapped himself around Cody, and he was grateful for this precious little man.

"I love you, Keata." Cody rolled to his side, Keata clinging to him. He couldn't believe the emotions that tore from him while in his mate's arms. He would kill anyone and anything that ever attempted to take his love from him.

"Sleep, mate," Keata whispered into Cody's ear.

"Sleep," Cody repeated as he pulled the covers over them.

* * * *

Keata sat obediently on the bed as Cody ran a brush through his mate's long black hair. They had just showered after making love two more times that morning.

"What does Keata mean?" Cody asked as the soft hair flowed through his fingers.

"Mean blessed."

"It fits. You're my blessing." Cody kissed Keata's neck then pulled Keata into his arms. "Hungry?" Cody nibbled down his mate's neck. He couldn't seem to get enough of him. Three rounds since last night, and he was ready to go for a fourth. His mate had the softest skin imaginable. His mewls and pleas drove Cody wild. He thanked the fates that he hadn't screwed up his chance with this beauty.

Although he hadn't wanted to hurt his best friend, Keata was his heart and soul. He wouldn't have waited much longer.

Cody stared down at the scar on his mate's thigh. He remembered that night. He had gone out of his mind when Maverick told them that Keata and Oliver were under attack. Not even thinking twice, he had shifted and raced to his mate to find a damn rogue wolf trying to chew his mate's leg off. He shuddered at the thought.

"Yes."

"I take you to breakfast?" He wanted to show his mate off to the world. Pamper and spoil him rotten.

"Okay. I want smoothie and chicken strips." Keata pulled out of Cody's arms and got dressed as Cody did the same. He hated to see his mate cover that beautiful skin.

"You should have a more balanced breakfast, Keata."

Keata narrowed his eyes on Cody. "'Cause you get this." He pointed to his butt. "No mean you tell me what I eat."

Cody's jaw fell to his chest. "What's wrong, Keata?"

"Want smoothie and chicken strips," Keata repeated.

"Bacon and eggs."

"Get what I want or you no get this no more." Keata turned and wiggled his ass, laughing as he ran out of the bedroom.

"Brat."

They made it downstairs holding hands as Kyoshi and Storm came through the front door.

"How's my favorite cousin?" Kyoshi smiled at Keata.

"Only cousin, silly." Keata slapped Kyoshi playfully on his chest.

"Still favorite." Kyoshi turned to Cody. "You guys heading out? Kinda nippy today."

"I'm taking my baby to breakfast." Cody helped Keata into his coat as he led him to the door. He wondered how many chicken strips the restaurant had.

"Have fun." Kyoshi waved as Cody led his mate to his truck, lifting Keata up and placing him in his seat. He reached over and buckled his mate in, kissing him on the tip of his nose before shutting the door. Cody walked around the front of the truck chuckling. He was such a goner. Keata had him wrapped around his finger, and the little guy didn't even know it, or did he?

Cody pulled in front of the diner, helping Keata down from the truck. He stopped when he saw the closed sign still hanging in the window. It was still early, but the diner should have been opened by now. Other people saw the sign and shook their heads as they walked away.

He didn't like this. Something was wrong. "Get back in the truck, Keata. Now," Cody ordered his mate.

Keata ran and pulled the door open, slamming it and engaging the locks, a frightened look on his face.

Cody smelled smoke as he looked to the side of the building. He heard a moan then a growl. Shit, he needed to get back there but feared leaving Keata by himself since the vampires were discovered so close by, especially after the way Christian had roamed his eyes over his mate.

He pulled his cell phone from his leather jacket and called Maverick, telling him of the situation.

"I'm sending help now."

"I have Keata with me. I can't leave him."

"Understood. Just stand down. Someone will be there shortly."

Cody slid his phone back into his jacket as a human emerged from behind the building, bloody and crying out for help. Cody looked back at his truck to see Keata covering his mouth and pointing at the bloody mess of a man.

"Stay," Cody shouted at Keata as he ran to the guy.

"Help me, please." He held his hand around his waist, and Cody saw blood seeping out from under the man's arm.

Two wolves came around the corner, coming to a halt when they saw Cody. They began to growl and snap their jaws.

"No, you fucking didn't just challenge me." Cody shifted and attacked, killing them both.

He shifted back and grabbed the remains of his favorite leather. Dammit, why couldn't wolves shift back and forth with their clothes? He went through more jackets than a department store. He pulled his phone out once more, calling the fire department and ambulance. He quickly ran to his truck, opening the silver box bolted to the bed. As a shifter, he had learned, along with the other wolves, to carry spare clothes. Tossing the jeans on, Cody quickly shoved his feet into boots and tossed a T-shirt over his head. Checking inside his truck to assure himself his mate was safe, Cody ran back to the human.

Murdock and Gunnar raced toward him in their truck. They grabbed the two wolves, looking around to make sure no humans saw them, and then tossed the carcasses into the bed.

Cody nodded as the Sentries sped off to remove evidence of their existence.

"What are you?" The man stared up at Cody, his brows furrowed.

"The man that decides whether you live or die for witnessing a well-guarded secret." Cody glared down at the man.

"I won't tell. I swear. I've seen you guys come into my diner plenty of times. I like you all. Never any problems. Good business." The man grunted at the pain he was experiencing.

"You the owner of the diner?" Cody thought he had looked familiar.

"Yeah, promise I won't tell. Name's Frank Thomas." He held a bloody hand up to Cody.

Cody eyes him wearily then shook the offered hand. "Cody Wilder. I'll be watching you, Frank Thomas."

"No problem. You know where I work." He tried to laugh, but it came out as a groan.

The fire truck pulled up along with the ambulance. Cody backed up and allowed the paramedics to work on Frank.

"Can you tell us what happened?" one of the medics asked Frank.

Frank looked over at Cody for a moment then back to the man

questioning him, "I was trying to get in through the back door when I was attacked by a dog, must be rabid. The fire started because I was smoking when it happened."

Cody nodded. "I'm his friend, Cody. This is Frank Thomas, owner of the diner. Where are you taking him?"

"Over to the Medic Center." The paramedic pulled Frank onto the stretcher and loaded him into the back of the ambulance.

"See you at the Medic Center, Frank Thomas." Cody turned his back and headed to his truck. Keata was watching the chaos in front of him with wide eyes.

Chapter Seven

Keata set the bottle back under the bar and ran around to sit on the couch next to Johnny. They both giggled as they sat there, watching Storm come into the den.

Keata had to bite his knuckle to stop the laughter as Storm went behind the bar, grabbed a beer bottle, twisted the cap off, and took a large swallow.

Storm spit out the drink, it sprayed across the bar as he wiped his tongue on his shirt. "What the fuck is this?"

Johnny giggled. Keata elbowed him to be quiet. Storm shot an angry look over at the two, but Keata curled his lips in and darted his eyes around.

Storm sniffed the bottle and then glared at them. "Who put Worcestershire sauce and vinegar in this bottle?"

Keata shrugged. "Beer bandit."

Johnny giggled again, and Keata almost burst out laughing.

"I'm going to go have a talk with Hawk and Cody." He pointed to the pair. "Stay away from the beer."

Keata watched Storm walk away, and then he and Johnny fell over laughing.

"That was a good idea." Johnny snorted.

"Yeah, good." Keata held his side as he laughed.

Storm came back in and stood there glaring at them. Keata rolled over and laughed harder. Johnny laughing so much, he was crying.

He needed a good laugh after what he witnessed this morning. It was enough to make him never want to leave the house again. Since Keata knew he couldn't live his life as a hermit, he dealt with it in his own way.

* * * *

Cody led Keata through the emergency room, asking to see Frank. The nurse led him to one of the rooms in the back.

He pushed the door open, seeing Frank lying on a bed, bandages covering him. "How ya feeling, Frank?"

"Like roadkill." He chuckled.

Keata walked over to the bed, but Cody pulled him back. "No, Keata. Man hurt."

Frank looked down at Keata. "He's beautiful."

"He's mine." Cody pulled Keata to his chest, a low growl vibrating from him.

Frank threw his hands up. "No harm meant, just complimenting your man."

"You gay?" Cody questioned him.

"No, but my brother is. I have no problem with gay people." Frank smiled warmly down at Keata.

"No problem." Keata grinned.

Frank began to speak to Keata in Japanese. Keata and Cody's eyes widened.

"My grandmother was from Japan and insisted I learn the language of my ancestors." Frank patted Keata on the back of his hand.

Cody growled again, and Keata tapped his chest. "Behave, mate."

Cody's eyes softened on Keata.

"So what are you?" Frank asked.

"I think you already know the answer to that question."

"Yeah, okay. So what's this mate thing your boyfriend is talking about?" Frank asked.

"You know if I tell you and you betray—"

Frank held his hand up. "I know you don't know me, but I like our little town. If the world found out about you...well, military and reporters everywhere." Frank shuddered. "No thanks."

"Well, it's about the same as mating in the animal world. One mate for life, and since I'm two hundred and seventy-two years old, living to be a thousand, that's a mighty long time to be alone."

"Holy shit!" Frank covered his mouth with his hand, looking at the door to make sure no one heard him. "You're older than me." Frank laughed.

Keata started laughing, too. "Old man." He snorted.

"I'll give you old." Cody pulled Keata into his arms and kissed him. He turned back to Frank, "So why did those"—Cody turned back to look at the door—"*men* attack you?"

"Don't know. I was honest when I said I was trying to get through the back door when they attacked, never seen them before."

"I'll inform my Alpha that they're attacking humans now." Cody couldn't figure out why the rogues would attack humans. What was there to gain? He knew rogues cared nothing for packs, cared nothing for keeping their secret. That's what made them dangerous, aside from the fact they were out to kill, but they usually kept it to other shifters.

Maverick was going to shit kittens on this one.

"There are more of you?" The human's eyes widened.

"A whole pack. Two, actually."

"Huh." Frank looked thoughtful.

"Listen, about your diner. I want to make it up to you for what those *men* did to you."

Frank held up his hand, "No, that's what I have insurance for."

"Insurance won't get you a brand-new, updated kitchen." Cody dangled the carrot in front of him.

Frank shook his head. "I can't allow you to come out of pocket."

"Before you say no again, we have more money than we know what to do with. Living as long as we have, it's no sweat off of our backs to help out. Give back to the community." This Frank guy was a tough sell. Any other human would jump at the chance of free money. He liked Frank's ethics.

"I don't care about your money. I'll tell you what. You can modernize my kitchen if you agree to become my partner in business."

Cody's eyes widened. "You mean it? I've never owned a business before." The idea had merit. It made him feel accomplished. Cody began to imagine what he wanted the place to look like. The excitement started building in him, but he kept a cool composure. There was one person, or he should say wolf, that had to approve this, and finding out that a human now knew they existed just might be the toughest sale yet compared to convincing the human to take the money.

Maverick had to agree.

This might have just gotten more complicated than Cody had anticipated.

"Only way I'll let you pay for the renovations."

"Deal." Cody shook Frank's hand. "But those damn wolves in my pack don't get to eat for free. The profit and pantry would be dry before the ink on our agreement was." Cody laughed.

"Deal, but you can't stop me from giving them free desserts." Frank winked at Keata.

Cody growled again.

"Will you stop that snarly thing? I don't want your mate. He's just so adorable." Frank waved his hand at Cody.

Cody was amazed at how well Frank was taking things. "I told you, one mate per lifetime."

"So how do you know who your mate is?" Frank was once again intrigued.

"You don't. You have to find them. Once you do, heaven or hell won't stop a wolf from claiming what's his. You just know, you know?" And thank goodness he hadn't blown his chance with Keata.

"Yeah, I knew Emma was mine from the first moment I laid eyes on her. I know what you mean, Cody." Frank's eyes misted.

"You married?"

"Widowed. My Emma was taken from me a few years back. Cancer." Frank wiped the stray tear that came from bringing up an obvious painful memory.

"Sorry, man." Cody couldn't imagine Keata being taken from him. Just the thought made his chest ache. He'd been a fool in waiting those months. But now that his mate was at his side, only the act of god could separate them.

"Let's leave the emotional stuff for the women and talk turkey. You come see me when I get out of here and we'll hash over all the details." Frank raised his hand to shake Cody's.

"Sounds good, Frank Thomas." Cody shook the hand.

Frank spoke to Keata in his own language again, getting a laugh from his friendly—*too friendly*—mate.

"What are you telling my mate?" Cody eyed Frank then Keata.

"That he has a smart wolf for a mate." Frank winked a Keata again.

Cody growled again.

Frank waved Cody's threat away. "No worries, old man." Frank chuckled.

Cody rolled his eyes and bid his farewells as he led Keata out of the Medic Center and drove him home.

* * * *

"Do you trust this Frank Thomas?" Maverick sat back in his chair, pulling at his soul patch. Interesting. He hadn't seen this one coming. So a human knew of their existence now.

"I do. He seemed cool about it, even offered me partnership in his diner for helping to renovate it. The fire destroyed the old one." Cody leaned back in the leather chair.

"I'll trust your instincts on this, but be aware, Sentry, if he betrays us, life as we know it won't exist anymore, and we'll be hunted."

Maverick knew he was taking a big risk at letting this human live, but it actually felt kind of nice for someone else to know and accept them. If Frank betrayed them, he would kill him slowly and painfully. Cecil's happiness and well-being came before even his own pack. He wasn't going to be on the run with his mate. *Ever.*

"I'll take full responsibility for him."

Maverick sat forward, looking the warrior straight in his eyes. "You know what you're saying, right? If this Frank does reveal our secret, you'll be killed along with him." Maverick wasn't going to pull any punches. Cody had to know what he was agreeing to.

"I know, and I don't take it lightly, Alpha."

"Very well, I would like to meet Frank Thomas and reserve judgment for myself. If I feel he isn't a threat, he lives, as do you." Maverick dismissed Cody.

* * * *

Cody hadn't expected that. He couldn't even warn his new partner. If he did, Maverick would skin Cody alive. His loyalties lay with his pack, but he had an urge to protect Frank. Maybe it was because the guy had stayed true to his word, not telling a soul, maybe because he felt for the widower. Maybe Keata's naïve trust was eroding Cody's damn brain.

* * * *

He found his mate licking a spoon he had just dipped into an ice cream container. Cody shook his head. All the mates should be five hundred pounds by now, but luckily they were young and had high metabolisms. That and the fact that being mated to a wolf burned off excessive fat. Something in their saliva was transmitted to their mates.

Cody chuckled as he thought how people across the globe would love to get their hands on the wolves' saliva, the new and improved

ground his cock into Keata's clothed ass.

"I want you, Cody." Keata moaned.

Cody smiled. "Very good. You remembered."

"Yes, remember." Keata pushed his ass down toward his hard cock, signaling to Cody that his mate wanted to feel it inside of him.

Cody had been working with Keata to teach him better English and, in turn, Keata had been teaching Cody basic Japanese.

"*Watashi was anata o aishite,*" Cody murmured.

"Very good. You remember." Keata smiled. "I love you, too."

"I got it right?" Cody was amazed he remembered. Keata had taught him only that morning.

"Yes. Now, no talk. Sex."

Cody burst out laughing, lifting Keata from his waist. "Strip."

Keata and Cody got naked then Cody lay back onto his back. "Ride me, Keata."

"No understand." Keata stood there with his hands clasped in front of him, shivering from excitement and the cold outside.

"Come here, I'll show you." Cody pulled Keata back onto his lap, positioning his legs.

"Oh, I see." Keata leaned forward as Cody stretched him. He'd been shocked to find lube in his coat pocket. Keata must have put it there when he grabbed their coats. So his mate must be just as addicted to their lovemaking as Cody was. He was glad Keata had taken the initiative. His mate didn't seem so scared of sex now.

"Glad you see." Cody moaned as his third finger sunk into Keata's tight entrance. He pulled his hand free and tapped Keata's hip. "Lift."

Keata lifted his ass, and Cody grabbed his cock, holding it in place as Keata slowly lowered. "So…so much."

"You mean full?" Cody held Keata's hips to help him steady himself.

"Yes, full. Like belly when too much food in." Keata smiled down at Cody.

Cody chuckled. "Yeah, full belly." He began to move Keata up and down on his shaft, thrusting his hips to meet him on every down stroke.

"I got." Keata dug his nails into Cody's chest and planted his feet, moving to the rhythm Cody had showed him.

"Fuck, you got all right." Cody slid his hands under his mate's small rounded globes as he locked eyes on him. Keata blushed at Cody's intense stare. He had never seen anything more breathtakingly beautiful then his mate riding him. The ecstasy on Keata's face drove him to the edge fast.

His hand reached up and pushed his mate's gorgeous, silky, hair from his face. He tucked it behind Keata's ear. Keata's lips parted, and Cody grabbed his mate's cock, pumping it until Keata stilled then cried out Cody's name.

Cody took over the thrusting. His hands landed on his mate's hips and pulled him up and down until Cody cried his name. Keata dug into Cody's flesh as his cock throbbed its release in Keata's ass. Cody was mindless with the raw feeling of protecting this little man.

"Cold." Keata panted as he fell onto Cody's chest.

Cody wrapped his arms around his mate, kissing the top of his head, never wanting to let him go. Reluctantly, he did. "Get dressed."

Keata climbed off and pulled his clothes on. Cody watched as his mate's flawless skin was covered.

"Food." Keata dropped down onto the blanket next to him. He grabbed another chicken strip and began to nibble on it.

He smiled at the basic needs his mate had. Keata wasn't complicated. He wasn't very hard to figure out. He showed Cody everything he was feeling and told him exactly what he was thinking.

Once he was dressed, Cody pulled his mate into his arms and hugged him close. He'd kill anyone who would try to take him away.

Chapter Eight

Keata wandered around the game store in town. Cecil had pleaded with Maverick to bring them here, saying they had mastered all the other games and needed new ones. Keata picked up a magazine with Asian characters on the front. He flipped through, reading the story.

He would ask Cody to buy it for him. He never asked his mate to buy things for him because Keata wasn't sure if his mate was poor like he and Kyoshi had been in Japan. The wolves didn't seem to be, but you never knew.

Keata browsed through a few more, selecting three in all. He hoped it wasn't too expensive.

"Excuse me? Cody needs you outside. He's hurt."

Keata snapped his head up to see a stranger standing next to him. He looked around but didn't see any mates or warriors around. Keata rushed outside to find his wolf. If his Cody was hurt, Keata had to help.

A hand slapped over his mouth as Keata neared the parking lot. He struggled, but the hand stayed firmly over him. He was tossed into a van, and then the door slammed shut. Keata began to panic. He wanted his Cody.

* * * *

"Keata!" Cody screamed at the top of his lungs. His mate had disappeared from the game store, and Cody was going ballistic. He tore the store apart, screaming over and over again for his mate.

"You have to find him!" he yelled at the warriors. He pulled at his hair as his chest felt like it was caving in.

* * * *

"We'll find him, Cody." Tank took off out the door, searching for any trail he could find. He was in a panic as well. Keata meant the world to him, and he was going to tear that damn world apart until the little guy was found.

"Anything?" Loco asked as he ran up to him.

"No." Tank punched the side of the building, the concrete crumbling under his assault.

"We've got to find him, Tank. He's too innocent. I don't think I couldn't live with myself if anything happened to him," Loco said.

"I know." Tank breathed out deeply. "Who the fuck took him?"

"Vamps? Rogues? Humans? I just don't know." Loco scanned the area as Cody burst from the store, his eyes darting wildly, looking for his mate.

"You have to—" A sob tore from Cody. "You have to find him." He ran off, shifting in the middle of the parking lot. Tank and Loco looked around to see if anyone had witnessed it, but the lot was empty.

"I think Cody will go rogue if we don't find Keata." Tank rubbed his hands over his head.

"No doubt."

* * * *

Keata whimpered when he saw the ugly American that had stolen him and Kyoshi and brought them to America.

"I knew I would eventually get you back. I lost three good rent boys because of your friends. You'll help pay for the lost money that all of you should have brought in." The ugly American slapped Keata across the face.

Keata held in a cry. He wasn't going to let these men know how scared he was.

"You are a pretty one. Top dollar will be paid for you." The ugly American lifted a piece of Keata's hair in his hand, rubbing it along his face.

Keata yanked his head back, not wanting anyone but Cody to touch him.

"Feisty, too." The man laughed. He yanked Keata closer, licking his tongue up the side of Keata's face.

Keata dry heaved. His skin was on fire from the touch. He wanted to scrub his face with a harsh pad.

Keata pushed from the man's arms as he felt the vehicle slowing down and then stopping.

"What the fuck are you doing?" The ugly American yelled at the driver.

"Not me. Someone's blocking the road up ahead."

"Well, go around them, dammit."

"Kinda can't."

Keata watched in horrified awe as the driver cursed and then was yanked out of the window.

He tried to push away from the ugly American to hide but he wouldn't release him, he struggled and was finally let go.

"What the hell?" The ugly American's eyes widened as he looked all around. The doors on the van flew off the hinges, and the ugly man was pulled out.

Keata crawled under the seat and cringed. His whole body was shaking, fearing he would be next to get pulled from the van. Where was Cody?

"Do not fear me." Keata heard a soft and reassuring voice. "Come, beautiful. I will not harm you."

Keata peeked from under the seat to see the man from the club. His fear skyrocketed. He knew this man wanted to take him from his Cody. Keata shook his head and pushed further under the seat. How did the ugly Americans find him, and how did the vampire find him?

"Come, precious. I will return you to your wolf. Promise." The vampire held out his hand.

Keata peeked from under the seat as the vampire smiled at him. He knew that look. It was the same one his Cody gave him when he wanted to have sex. Keata was terrified to leave his refuge.

The vampire knelt down. "You are truly breathtaking. I have never before seen a man so innocent. So stunning."

With a whimper, Keata reached his trembling hand out and laid it in the vampire's. He knew he couldn't stay under the seat. He knew Christian had him. Keata just prayed Christian was telling the truth and would return him.

"That's right, beautiful. Come to me." The vampire pulled Keata into his arms, hugging him closely. Keata didn't want the man to touch him, although he did smell really good. "What is your name, precious?"

"K–Keata."

"A beautiful name for a beautiful man." The vampire carried Keata over to his car, sliding in the backseat with Keata still in his arms. "I will take you to my home—"

Keata cried out and tried to push away. "Promise. You promise."

"Settle, little one. Yes, I promised, and I will return you. I must have your Alpha come to me to retrieve you. I don't want the wolves attacking me or my men thinking we had anything to do with this." The vampire petted Keata's hair.

"Promise?"

"Yes, little one."

Keata relaxed a little. There went his stupid trust again, but the vampire seemed sincere.

Keata pulled until the vampire let him go. He slid onto the seat and pulled his legs up to his chest. His belly was starting to hurt. He had missed lunch, and now his belly was complaining. Keata stared out of the window as Brac Village began to disappear, his anxiety making him tremble.

He wanted Kyoshi and all the friends he made at his new home, and wondered if he and Johnny would ever be able to play another prank again. But most of all he wanted his Cody.

They pulled into a long driveway. Keata whimpered when the vampire opened the back door for him to get out.

"I will not harm you, little one."

Keata slid from the back seat then turned to close the door. He was trying his best to be brave as he followed the vampire into his house. A sharp pain cut across Keata's belly. He stumbled then fell to the ground crying out.

"What is it, little one?"

"Belly. Hurt." Keata's arms began to shake. He rolled over to his side, the pain tearing through him. He was vaguely aware of arms pushing under him then lifting him up.

* * * *

Christian paced in his manor. What was he supposed to do? He knew he promised Keata that he would return him, but he hadn't expected the beauty to start screaming in pain.

His best bet was to call the Alpha, tell him where Keata was, and let him deal with it, but his heart was agonizing over the cries of pain coming from his bedroom. He had placed the little human in there when he started crying and holding his midsection.

To hell with it. He had to call. Maybe they knew what was going on.

Christina took a deep breath and flipped his cell phone open. This was going to be as fun as trying to suck blood from a corpse.

* * * *

"Maverick."

"I believe I have something that belongs to you," Christian said.

"Where is he?" Maverick growled into the phone.

"Who? Who has Keata? I want him back! If you fucking harm him, I will hunt you down and eat your damn entrails," Cody screamed as Tank and Loco grabbed him by his arms.

They had gathered in Maverick's office to devise a plan to find Keata when the phone had rang.

"I thought you said the mates were safe?" Maverick barked out.

"And they are. I want you to be aware that I had absolutely nothing to do with this, nor did my men. Some slimy, fat human took him. I was on my way to see you when I witnessed the kidnapping."

"Why not bring him right back to us if that were the case?" Maverick questioned.

"Right. Do you see how his mate is acting now? Even I can hear him. I would have been attacked before one word left my lips. This was a safer route. Come claim him. I don't need the headache." Christian hung up the phone.

"Christian has him."

"I'll fucking kill him." Cody howled as he ripped his arms from the warriors' tight hold.

"Stop!" Maverick barked out in his commanding voice.

Cody stopped at the door he was running to. "Why? If it were Cecil, nothing would stop you."

"Agreed, but you must know that Christian saved him from some humans that had originally taken him." God, even Maverick had a hard time swallowing that story.

"Not likely. I saw the way he looked at my Keata in the club. He wants him. I don't know what game he's playing, but I'll kill him before I allow him to get at Keata again." Cody's canines descended as his eyes glowed crimson.

"We ride. Bring Kyoshi. Keata is going to need him." Maverick waved them to the door.

"If something happens to my mate, I'll kill everyone in sight. No discriminating, vamp or wolf," Storm warned them all.

"Noted." Maverick ordered Evan and Murdock to stay behind and guard the other mates with their lives.

"Yes, Alpha," Murdock and Evan said in unison.

* * * *

They rode fourteen deep, including Kyoshi, who shook in Storm's arms. He had been crying since Keata disappeared.

"Shush, dragonfly. We're going to get him now." Storm rubbed Kyoshi's back.

"What if he was harmed? What if they did unspeakable things to him? I couldn't live with the knowledge that I failed him." Kyoshi grabbed Storm's shirt and cried harder.

"You didn't fail him, little one. No one did. Just believe he is fine." Storm prayed he was right because he was beating himself up over this as well. They all were. All the wolves blamed themselves for Keata leaving their sight. How the hell did Christian get Keata out of the store with no one seeing?

They pulled in front of a manor between their small town and the city. Storm also wondered how they were able to come out in daylight. Maybe all the myths weren't true.

* * * *

"Cody, I warn you. I want to hear what Keata says before I step aside and let you tear the prince apart. We have to know for sure before we start a war," Maverick warned Cody.

What the fuck ever. "Sure." Cody jumped from the SUV. He was wearing fatigue pants strapped with knives. He was a wolf, able to kill anyone, but he wasn't sure how to kill a vampire, so he took extra precautions.

Cody kicked the front door with his combat boot, slamming the bottom of his foot into the wood. "Give me my goddamn mate now!"

"Cody!" Maverick admonished him

The front door opened, and the small man stepped aside as Cody raced in. "Keata!" Cody screamed, pacing back and forth in the foyer.

Chills ran down his spine at the silence. The small man waved for them to follow him. Cody pulled a large, serrated knife from its sheath, holding it in his hand as he readied himself.

The small man took them down a flight of stairs, and Cody watched everything around him.

"This better not be a trap," Maverick warned.

"It is not, sir. You will find the young Keata unharmed." The man waved his hand at a large black shiny door. It looked solid and heavy. Something a vampire would use to keep unwanted guests out. Cody shoved it open, running to the large, four-poster bed Keata was laying on, crying out for him. "He's going through the change, just as Kyoshi did." Cody gasped.

"We have no herbs here." Maverick paced back and forth.

"What's the likelihood of both cousins going through the change? Something isn't adding up." Cody crawled on the bed, massaging his mate even without the lotion used for easing the pain of a shifters transition. Keata cried as tiny claws emerged from his hands. Cody knew there was a chance Keata may not make it through the change. He could lose his mate. Cody cried as he rocked Keata in his arms. He couldn't lose him.

"I had nothing to do with this," Christian informed them when he entered the room.

"Get the fuck out of here!" Cody yelled.

"No, he save." Keata panted. "Ugly American take."

"Do you have herbs around here?" Maverick turned to the prince.

"No, but I can send my men to obtain whatever it is you need." Christian snapped his fingers, and two vampires appeared. "Tell them what you need."

Maverick named the herbs, and the vampires bowed before taking off.

"How is it that you can go out in daylight?" Gunnar asked.

"Myth, although we cannot be out in it too long or we get a nasty sunburn. Fair skinned, you know." Christian looked over at Keata. "What is wrong with him? I brought him in here to make him more comfortable but was at a loss to know what to do for him."

"He's shifting for the first time." Maverick watched Keata. Everyone was worried for him.

"Into a wolf?"

"I'm afraid that is all I am at liberty to tell you." Maverick shrugged his shoulders then turned to Cody.

Cody knew his Alpha wasn't going to give the prince any more information than he needed. They needed to get Keata out of here before the change. They didn't want anyone knowing that the small Asian was about to become a tiger. They were extremely rare, and Kyoshi's secret was well guarded. No one, not even the Eastern pack, was aware that there was a cat shifter at the estate. Now his mate would be guarded as well.

The men returned with the herbs. Maverick thanked them and ordered Cody to wrap his mate up and take him out to the waiting SUV.

"But it could be dangerous for him," Cody protested, massaging Keata's limbs. He knew they had to leave but feared the trip would kill Keata. He was torn.

"We will make it fast, but we must leave." Maverick's voice brooked no argument.

Cody wrapped Keata up in the silk comforter before pushing past everyone and running up the stairs.

"I would not have told his secret," Christian informed the Alpha.

"Duly noted. Thank you for helping him." Maverick shook his hand before the warriors ran after Cody.

Chapter Nine

Cody rubbed aloe vera lotion into Keata's skin. The entire pack was in his room watching the shift. His mate lay naked under a sheet as he rubbed his sore limbs.

Since Kyoshi had gone through the same change, they knew what to expect. It still didn't make watching it any easier. The wolf physician had met them at the house, taking blood samples at Maverick's request, the Alpha wanting to know why cousins who did not share the same father both had shifter blood flowing in their veins.

"I found your answer." The doctor looked up from his microscope he had brought with him along with other various machines at the Alpha's request. "They share the same DNA, but not as cousins. As brothers."

"How?" Kyoshi cried out. Storm had to hold his mate up as Kyoshi stumbled backward.

"Same father." The doctor turned back to his work.

"Could our mothers not have known?" Kyoshi stared at Keata."I can't believe this. Brothers?"

Storm pulled Kyoshi into his arms, holding his mate close. Kyoshi stared opened mouth at Keata. Cody felt for Kysohi, but his concerns were with Keata right now.

"I remember the pain but not how long it took. Will he suffer much longer?" Kyoshi turned to Maverick.

"No, Kyoshi," Maverick assured him.

The tea had been brought in after brewing for an hour. Cody held his mate as Storm tipped the cup to his lips. Keata seemed to have quieted once he drank it. Cody worried. Keata was not acting the same as Kyoshi when he shifted.

"No two shifts are alike," Maverick reminded him.

Cody watched as Keata became the most beautiful tiger. His mate shifted flawlessly and lay on the bed staring up at him.

Cody crawled onto the bed, and Keata curled into his lap.

They all stared at the small tiger that lay in Cody's lap. Keata had survived the shift.

"Take him out, Cody. Let him run." Maverick waved everyone out.

He led his mate from the room, leaning down to scratch behind his ears. Keata had stopped a few times to bat at his hands.

When Johnny came running to his mate, Keata pounced on him and they rolled around.

"Now we can really pull some pranks," Johnny whispered, but Cody heard.

Cody shifted once they reached the backyard, Keata bouncing around as he played with him. Kyoshi shifted into his cat form as well.

The wolves all joined in, with Loco and Tank chasing after Keata, Cody growling and chasing after the wolves.

Keata rolled around on the grass, pawing at Cody.

Cody nipped at him and moved him toward the kitchen door after hours of play.

He took his mate upstairs, helping Keata to shift back to human form with Kyoshi's help. Cody wouldn't allow anyone else in the room considering Keata would be naked when he returned to his human form.

"My brother." Kyoshi cried as he held Keata.

"How?" Keata asked as he pulled away and dressed. He pulled Keata back into his arms, tears falling down his cheeks. Kyoshi began to cry, and Cody trotted into the bathroom to get dressed and give them a moment of privacy.

When he emerged, they were still hugging and crying.

"Same father, different mother," Kyoshi told Keata as he wiped the tears from his face.

"Then you two are still cousins. This is confusing." Cody petted Keata's back as he crawled into Cody's lap.

"I don't know how it all works, but that is true. I don't care. I still love Keata no matter what has changed." Kyoshi kissed Keata's cheek before leaving the room.

"Come here, kitty." Cody smiled as he pulled Keata closer to him, his cock hardening when Keata purred.

* * * *

Keata and Johnny snuck into Maverick's office.

Keata stuck the whoopee cushion on the Alpha's seat as Johnny smeared the face paint around the mouthpiece on the phone sitting on Maverick's desk.

They replaced his chai tea with black coffee and ran from the room.

"Maverick, can we talk to you?" Johnny asked innocently.

"Sure, fellas." Maverick led them into his office and took a seat.

Keata tried to keep a straight face as the loudest fart emanated from Maverick's chair. He looked up at the two, his brows pulled together.

"Uh, excuse me." Maverick turned to them, his cheeks blushing. "Now what did you two need?

"I was wondering if you could call Hawk for me. I just can't seem to find him anywhere."

Keata bit the inside of his mouth.

"Sure." Maverick picked the phone up and dialed, talking into the mouthpiece. When he hung up, Johnny and Keata couldn't stop the laughter at the face paint on Maverick's chin and lower lip.

Maverick growled and picked up his tea, spitting it out after taking a healthy swallow.

"Okay, you two have had your fun. Get out and go harass someone else."

The two raced from the room, peals of laughter following after them.

* * * *

Maverick sat back and chuckled. He had known what was going on, but why spoil their fun? He grabbed a napkin from his drawer and wiped his face off.

* * * *

Cody walked into the closed diner with Keata's hand held tightly in his.

He hadn't let Keata leave his side. "Frank?" Cody yelled out as he entered the place.

"Back here, Cody," Frank yelled out from past the gutted kitchen.

Cody led Keata to the back. He glanced around at what would need to be done to bring this place back to standards and codes to get it running again.

"Hey." Frank held his hand out to Cody, shaking it.

"I see I get to talk with my little friend as well." Frank patted Keata on the shoulder, ignoring Cody's growl.

Cody explained to him what happened a week ago. Keata's kidnapping, not the shifting part. It was decided that the less people knew about the tigers, the better.

"Fuck me, man. Did you kill the bastards?" Frank ruffled Keata's hair and offered him a smoothie, not knowing Keata went gaga over them.

"They will no longer be a problem." Cody leaned against a sawhorse.

"Good. All to hell with whoever tries to hurt the little guy." Frank waved Cody to his office, leaving the door open so Cody could watch Keata suck down the thick drink.

"You know, you just won him over. Smoothies and chicken strips are his all-time favorites." Cody chuckled as he watched his mate lovingly.

"Good to know." Frank slid the plans over to Cody. "Now, I've taken the liberty of pricing the new equipment and the labor of construction."

Cody looked at the pages of equipment Frank had printed out. "Won't do."

"What do you mean? It's great, sturdy equipment." Frank furrowed his brows.

"I don't want sturdy. Here." Cody pulled the large envelope from inside his jacket and slid it to Frank. "I also took the liberty of picking out new equipment. Although I'm no expert when it comes to what's needed in a kitchen, I'm sure I pretty much got what we need."

Frank pulled the papers from the envelope, his eyes bulging. "You've got to be kidding me? These are state of the art appliances, industrial size refrigerators and marble counter tops?" Frank looked up at Cody then back down at the pictures. "Is that a seventy-two inch wide, heavy duty restaurant range with twelve burners? Did you look at the price?" Frank opened his mouth then closed it again like a fish.

"I told you, price isn't a concern, and I don't want to hear an argument. If I'm going to be a partner, it's nothing but the best." Cody looked back at Keata before continuing. "I live a long time. I want to make sure I have enough savings for me and Keata to live off of, please understand." Cody implored.

"Is that really a triple glass and chrome refrigerator?"

"Yep, three swinging glass doors, nine shelves, and twenty-nine and a half inch depth, stores a lot of chicken strips in there." Cody smiled.

"I bet we could. Okay, you buy the equipment, and I'll oversee the construction." They shook hands one more time before Cody latched on to Keata.

Frank's eyes widened when Maverick stepped through the kitchen. "Frank Thomas, Alpha Maverick Brac." Cody stepped aside with Keata once he introduced the two. If he was going to kill Frank, he didn't want Keata close.

"Stay, Cody. You vouched for him, so you know the penalty if I disapprove." Maverick stepped to Frank as Cody released Keata, setting him on his feet and pushing his mate behind him.

"Keata is safe, Sentry." Maverick circled around Frank.

Cody watched as Frank's eyes widened, but he didn't attempt to run. The man must have known death stared him in the face, but he didn't flinch. He stayed still for the Alpha's inspection.

"Why should I trust you to keep our secret safe?" Maverick leaned over Frank, who was only five nine.

Cody saw the fear in Frank's eyes before he quickly masked it. Frank stood tall, taking a military stance. Cody was amazed that Frank looked like he would die proud if that's what was about to happen. "I am a man of honor. Cody saved my life and is offering to renovate my business."

"So this is about money?" Maverick stopped when he was behind Frank.

"Never. I refused him, but the man is too damn stubborn." Frank still didn't flinch when Maverick leaned even closer.

"Yes, Cody can be that." Maverick bared his canines, circling around for Frank to see.

"As I have told Cody, I like our small town, and I don't want military or reporters swarming the place." Frank gulped slightly when he saw Maverick's canines. Cody didn't blame him.

"So you say. Why should I let you or Cody live?" Maverick asked.

"Cody, sir?" Frank looked at Maverick with confusion.

"Yes, Cody. He vouched for you, so if I feel you're a threat, I eliminate both of you." Maverick backed off, staring Frank straight in his eyes, letting the crimson show.

"I don't know how to answer that, Alpha. Only that I repay what I owe, and I owe Cody my life."

Cody said a prayer, not sure that Frank convinced Maverick. He could feel Keata pulling on his shirt behind him. He knew his mate didn't understand what was going on, but you'd have to be blind not to see the threat the Alpha posed.

"Now your life belongs to me. Betray us, and it will be a long and agonizing death, Frank Thomas. There is nowhere you can hide." Maverick walked out of the gutted kitchen.

"Did I pass?" Frank looked over at Cody.

"Thank fuck." Cody blew out the breath he had been holding.

"Is that a yes? Because I need to know before I shit my pants." Frank smiled.

"That's a yes. But remember, if he even thinks you've betrayed us, you and I both will wish for death years before it comes."

"Years?" Frank gaped. "I'm not sure I want to know about wolves anymore.

"Years. Now, as I was saying…"

* * * *

Frank was floored at the grand reopening when so many wolves came in to eat. Cody had never mentioned how huge they all were. Even more amazing were the little guys hanging onto them. He recognized Keata and Cody, but the rest made his diner look like a kitchenette.

He also recognized Alpha Maverick. He had a small guy hugging him, which made the Alpha seem less intimidating. Maverick stared into the little guy's eyes like he was the only one in the world for him. Frank relaxed when Cody introduced him to the other Sentries. Frank was still trying to figure all of it out.

"I'm Tank." Tank stuck his hand out to Frank. "I'll be one of your best customers." He smiled.

"I recognize you." Frank laughed. "You order half the menu every time you come in."

"Growing pup has to eat." Tank slapped Frank on the back, damn near knocking him to the floor. "Shit, I'm sorry. I never had a human friend before, well, except for the mates. I forget my strength sometimes."

Frank stretched his back. "No worry, I'll send you the chiropractor's bill."

"Really?" Tank looked worried.

"Uh, no. Kidding." Frank shook his head. He liked Tank.

"Oh, okay then." Tank walked off.

"Great turnout." Cody walked over to him, shaking his hand.

"Great." Frank agreed.

Keata ran up to Frank, jumping around like a puppy. "Smoothie please."

"*Anata no tame ni mo, wakai yūjin.*" Frank smiled.

"What?" Cody looked at Frank.

"I said 'anything for you, young friend.'" He clapped Cody on his back.

"Better be all." Cody gave Frank the evil eye. Once again, Frank waved him off.

* * * *

"He really doesn't fear us?"

Cody looked over his shoulder to see Maverick standing behind him.

"He fears. Just won't show it," Cody explained.

"Hmm." Maverick walked over to Cecil and pulled him in his lap. Cody understood where Maverick was coming from just by watching him with his mate, still.

* * * *

Frank stepped out of the kitchen. "Cody, we have a problem."

Frank stepped back as the entire room surrounded him.

"What's wrong?" Tank looked over Frank's shoulder.

Frank took a deep breath and shook his head, waving his arms. "No, not that kind of problem. My cook just quit, says he ain't cooking all this damn food."

"Want me to go convince him?" Tank offered.

"You'd do that?" Frank looked up at Tank in amazement.

"Yeah, I like you. You feed me."

Frank burst out laughing, "Nice to know. No, Tank. I just need to hire a new one. Until then"—he turned to Cody—"you'll have to get hands on here."

Everyone groaned.

"He can't cook," one of the wolves yelled.

"Gonna have to for now." Frank chuckled.

"Got poison control on speed dial?" Remi asked.

"No, but since you suggested it…" Frank tried to hide his laugh.

"Hey," Cody snarled at Frank.

"No snarling." Keata patted Cody's chest. Cody looked down at his mate with nothing but love in his eyes.

Frank was amazed at the depth to which these wolves loved their mates. He would forever keep their secrets with the new friendships he just formed.

THE END

LYNNHAGEN@YAHOO.COM

GEORGE'S TURN

LYNN HAGEN

SIREN
Publishing

Everlasting Classic

The
ManLove
Collection

BRAC PACK 8

GEORGE'S TURN

Brac Pack 8

LYNN HAGEN
Copyright © 2011

Chapter One

George pulled his truck into the space in front of the diner. He cut the engine and just sat there and stared. The diner was small as one would expect in a small town. There was a post office to the right of it. The building sat on the corner of a tiny strip of businesses.

"This is a far cry from Wyoming," he muttered, wondering if he could do this. He was a damn cowboy. What business did he have coming out here to take a job as a cook in a small-town diner? His cousin Leon had called him about the opening, and George had jumped at the opportunity, but now that he was here, he was second-guessing his decision. He wasn't so sure he could do this.

He had grown up on a ranch and worked on one since he was old enough to walk. George thought about the last ranch he worked on as a ranch hand. This made him think of Jesse. His heart clenched at the thought of his ex-lover. George had been kicked off of two previous ranches when the others found out he was gay. He thought he had finally found a home at the Triple R.

He had to sneak around for a year with the handsome cowboy, Jesse, who swore his undying love to George. His heart was ripped clean from his chest when the other hands had found out George's sexual preference and confronted him. He expected Jesse to stand by his side. Instead, the man had faded into the shadows like a thief in the night with George's heart.

George pushed the memory back as he opened the door to his truck, reaching over and grabbing his cowboy hat, slapping it on his thigh to rid it of the Wyoming dust that still clung to it. Placing it on his head, he sauntered over to the quaint little diner and headed in.

George sat at one of the stools at the counter, looking around the place. It seemed pretty empty. His cousin Leon knew he had a passion for cooking, so he figured this would be the perfect place for George to start a new life. A clean break. All he had to do was make sure nobody found out he was gay.

He wasn't sure if he could stay stationary for so many hours behind a hot grill, though, after roping cattle and the day-to-day life of a hardworking ranch hand. This…this was the polar opposite.

"Can I help you?" A young woman smiled from behind the counter.

"I'm here to see Frank Thomas." George mentally rolled his eyes when the waitress winked at him. She was nice enough looking for a female. Big, wide hips that probably gave birth to a few rug rats, large swollen breasts and way too much lipstick and makeup. Her eyes looked like she just stuck her face in the makeup case and shook it. Without all the gunk, she was probably pretty.

He liked the body under him flat-chested and lean with muscles. Unfortunately, he got this reaction everywhere he went. Women—and some men—threw themselves at him. Jesse had told him that he had the prettiest blue eyes and the softest blond hair. George's lips thinned with anger as he thought of the man who still held his heart. No more. He wasn't going to play the fool for anyone anymore. Some said he was blessed with good looks, but George knew it to be a curse.

Jesse had sworn he loved him and would always be there for him. George had trusted Jesse, gave him his heart, and the man had shredded it into a thousand pieces. Bastard.

George leaned his elbows onto the counter, pulling at the beard of his goatee while he waited on Frank to appear from wherever he was.

All he wanted was a warm place to lay his head and a steady job. No drama, no confrontations, and definitely no more men. He felt old for his twenty-eight years, having been through too much in such a short time.

He had told his dad he wanted to be a chef then got his head slapped, his dad yelling at him that cooking was for females and he needed to get his ass outside and get the cow milked. His father was a big time homophobic. There was no *coming out* in Wyoming. Not if you wanted to survive after your declaration.

"You must be George Knight." A stout man came from behind the chrome double doors with his hand extended.

"Yes, sir," George shook his hand as he stood, "and you must be Mr. Thomas."

"Call me Frank. I see you met Kitty." Frank nodded toward the waitress.

"Yes, I've met her." George ignored the lustful winks. With all that makeup on, she was probably just trying to dislodge the goop.

"Do you have any experience cooking? Leon wasn't too clear on that." Frank waved George to the back. He sidestepped the waitress, trying to keep his body parts away from her as she brushed her hand close to his rear end.

"Some. I like to cook. Cooked on the ranch and got pretty good at it." George immediately took in the updated kitchen, with a twelve-burner stove and large ovens. There were wide sinks and a commercial-size refrigerator with three glass doors. Damn, this was nice.

"As you can see, everything has been updated. I recently renovated. Business isn't that good, if that's what you're thinking. Someone donated the money for the renovation." Frank waved him into a small back office, then he handed George the necessary paperwork to fill out. He sat there and completed it as Frank continued to talk.

"I have a studio apartment upstairs you can rent out. Leon tells me you come from Wyoming. Must be a culture shock going from a ranch to a small town. We aren't as populated as the city, but we do get a lot of tourists who pass through." Frank filed away his paperwork and took George back to the kitchen he'd be working in.

"Yeah, I reckon it's very different from the backwoods of the Triple R." George pushed his black Stetson hat back and scratched his head. He hoped it wasn't too big of a shock. He wanted nothing but peace and quiet. No drama. It wasn't that he was afraid. He'd fought his way out of many fights. At six three, he was no lightweight. He was just tired of having to fight.

"Well, I'll let you get acquainted with your new kitchen. I'll come get you around quitting time to show you the apartment. Get ready. Lunch rush will be coming soon." Frank slapped him on the back then left him alone.

George searched the kitchen for all the equipment he would need. He set the skillets out onto the stove along with the big pots.

"Your first order, hon." Kitty slid the order onto the counter, lingering just a bit as she watched George. He shrugged off her unwanted attention and grabbed the order, setting about cooking as the lunch rush got underway. Frank wasn't kidding. The place was packed.

He set a plate of fried chicken and mashed potatoes on the counter as he looked around the place, noticing a table with three large men sitting there. They were nice looking but not George's type. He liked his men slim and shorter than him, and being a very dominate male, he wanted submissive men. Jesse had been perfect. Too bad he was a cowardly prick.

George shook off the memory as he went back to cooking.

* * * *

Tank sat with Hawk and Kota. His Commander and Beta insisted he go to lunch with them. When they insisted, no one argued. They said that Alpha Maverick had one of his damn dreams again and sent them all to lunch on him. Ever since Maverick claimed his mate, Cecil, he had been having dreams occasionally, sending the Sentries off on missions with the end result that someone found a mate.

Tank looked around the diner, wondering if this was the case with him. With all the wolves finding mates left and right, he was more than hopeful his would be found soon. He wanted what he'd seen at home, the love and devotion the Timber wolves showered on the mates they had claimed. They seemed to walk around in a constant state of dreamy eyes.

He wanted that.

The waitress brought their food. Damn, the fried chicken looked good. It was nice and crispy, just the way he liked it. The mashed potatoes had a hint of garlic in them. Frank must have gotten the new cook he was looking for, and he had obviously hit the jackpot. With nobody at home to cook for the pack, they had to fend for themselves. It was nice to eat a good meal instead of frozen entrees or burnt noodles. He sucked at cooking.

Tank ate and ate a lot. At six seven and three hundred and twenty pounds, he damn near ate the pantry clean at home every day. Thank god he did patrol duty. Shifting into his wolf form, he ran for miles, working the calories off.

"The food is really good," Hawk commented as he dug into his plate. Tank was tempted to steal a piece of his steak tips but really liked having ten fingers. Maybe he would order some to go. He raised his hand to call the waitress over, putting in a to-go order of the steak tips, two burgers, another order of fried chicken and a spinach salad with grilled chicken. He would need a snack for later.

"Fuck, man, where do you put all of that?" Kota joked. "I need to put in an order of fried chicken for Blair. My sunshine needs lunch."

Hawk did the same for his mate, Johnny. The fried chicken seemed to be a big hit with everyone. Kota went ahead and ordered ten more fried chicken dinners for the other mates and their warriors at home and a chicken strip dinner for the Sentry Cody's mate, Keata. The man went gaga for chicken strips. He also remembered a smoothie for Keata as well. Although Cody was part owner of the diner, it was still nice to think of his mate when others were being taken care of.

Frank came out when the waitress had left them to place their to-go orders.

"Like the fried chicken, eh." He laughed.

"You must have that new cook. Everything was great." Hawk wiped his mouth as he stood halfway and shook Frank's hand.

"He just started today. Glad to see he's working out. Comes from Wyoming. Guess he's looking for a fresh start. Glad it's here." Frank gave the three free desserts. Cody had saved his life and helped renovate the new kitchen after the fire, becoming Frank's business partner. Cody insisted the hungry wolves pay for their meals, but Frank managed to bargain free desserts, at least for them. Tank was thankful for that and tried not to eat a whole cake himself. After all, he was a big man.

"Well, gentlemen, enjoy the rest of your meals. I look forward to seeing your mates."

"Maybe we'll bring them on our next visit." Kota shook Frank's hand as the stout man left them to eat. Frank knew of them being were-creatures. Cody had saved him from an attack of rogue wolves that had shifted right in front of Frank, attacking him and almost killing him.

"Damn, I'm still hungry," Tank complained. He eyed Hawk's plate once again. Hawk gave a low growl.

"Try it and get your hand stabbed," Hawk warned as he forked another tip and moaned as he chewed, teasing Tank.

"Dammit." Tank waved the waitress over and ordered a plate of the steak tips. "Give it to me rare and fast," he pleaded, his stomach rumbling in agreement.

* * * *

Who the hell was ordering all this fried chicken? George was barely keeping up. Another order of steak tips came in, and he tossed them on the grill with his secret seasonings and some onions. He dropped another batch of chicken in the fryer as he pulled a handful of the chicken strips out and dropped them as well. George grabbed a stack of to-go containers to put all the food in.

He tossed the spinach salad and sliced the grilled chicken to sprinkle over it, again adding his secret spices to the mix. He chopped the tomatoes, tossing them on top with crumbled blue cheese.

George slung container after container onto the counter as they became ready. He laid the plate of tips up there as well and watched Kitty carry it over to the table with the three large men. *Figures.* George watched in amazement as one of the men literally swallowed the whole plateful of tips. Holy crap!

Kitty came back and bagged the white Styrofoam containers, leaving them at the register. Well, what a surprise, the big fella paid and grabbed all the bags. If men like him came in here all the time, no wonder Frank had a new kitchen.

George cleaned up his mess as the rush receded. He wiped down his grill and counters, cleaning his equipment and stacking the dishes in the dishwasher.

Man, that was a hell of a first day. He prayed he could keep up with the dinner rush. If it was anything like lunch, then George knew he was going to be plumb tired by the time the diner closed.

"You wanna go out to the bar after work?" Kitty smiled at him from behind the counter. Shit. He didn't want to deal with this. Telling her he was gay would stop her in her tracks, maybe, but it would create a whole new set of problems he wasn't willing to deal with.

"I don't believe in mixing personal with business. We're

coworkers." That should get her off of his back.

"We can keep it separate. I promise." Kitty ran her tongue over her bottom lip, trying her best to entice him. George shuddered at the thought, no thanks.

"Sorry, can't. It's a rule I live by." So he was lying. She wouldn't know. Even if he slept with the opposite sex, Jesse had taught him a valuable lesson. Keep your heart and dick close. He didn't need the entanglement. He hadn't even been in town a whole day and already he was fighting for people to leave him the hell alone.

"Fine. Here's your next order." Kitty slapped the piece of paper onto the counter as she scowled at him. Rejection tended to make people a bit irritable. He would rather deal with irritability then horniness.

George grabbed the order and began the fries.

* * * *

The dinner rush was just as brutal. His fried chicken seemed to be a hit, and more orders for his homemade chili and steak tips came in as well. George was jumping around the kitchen, tossing chicken into the fryer, sautéing the tips, and stirring his chili. The cornbread came out of the oven a light golden brown. Perfect.

George had just tossed another plate up onto the window when he noticed one of the large men had returned, but now he had two smaller men with him. Was the guy always with someone new? George shook his head as he went back to his duties.

"Hey, George, I need to see you out here," Frank yelled from behind the counter.

Just great. George didn't have time to chat. He had cooking to do. Pulling the chicken out and laying the tips on a plate, George wiped his hands on his apron as he strolled out of the kitchen to see what Frank wanted.

"I want you to meet a friend of mine." Frank led him over to the big fella.

Fine. If Frank wanted to play politics, what could George really do about it? Say hello and get his ass back to the kitchen, that's what.

"George Knight, I'd like you to meet Tank Forney." Frank stepped back so George could shake hands.

Tank stared at George like he was an alien. He knew he was a mess from cooking all day, but he wasn't *that* bad.

Tank stood and let out a low growl. "Mine." He grabbed George's hand and pulled him into his arms.

"Whoa, partner. I'm not doing the two-step with ya." George pushed at Tank's chest, escaping his arms. What the hell did the guy think he was doing? He looked around to see who all had noticed another man hugging on him. His eyes darted around, but the other customers were busy eating. Thank goodness. He wasn't ready to pack up and run.

"But you're mine." Tank looked disheartened. George couldn't figure out what was going on here, but he didn't like it one bit. He turned back to the big man.

"I'm nobody's, least of all a man's. Nice meetin ya, Tank Forney." George nodded his head then went back to the kitchen. What the hell had gotten into that guy?

* * * *

"Is he really your mate, Tank?" Frank asked as he scratched his jaw.

"Yes." Tank dropped back down in the booth, his heart breaking in half. His mate didn't want him. Why would George reject him? Wasn't he pleasing to his mate?

"It'll be okay, Tank. I fought it at first, too. Give him time." Oliver patted Tank's hand.

"You did?" Tank felt a little hope spark inside him.

"Yeah, I didn't want anyone to know I was gay. You know, my

dad and all." Oliver lowered his head in shame.

"Thanks, Oliver, and your dad was an asshole, and we all know it. Hold your head up." Tank hated the fact that Oliver and his brother Blair were molested by their own damn father. He wanted to rip the man's sick and twisted heart out.

Oliver smiled and began eating again. "This fried chicken really is good. Your mate's a real good cook, so now maybe we'll get some decent meals at home"

"Nope, the steak tips are." Blair punched his brother in his shoulder.

"All right, you two. You need to eat up. Kota and Micah will start worrying if I don't get you back soon." Tank shoved another spoonful of mashed potatoes in his mouth as he watched the kitchen for any signs of his mate. The man was breathtaking. The cowboy was tall, handsome, with a beautifully proportioned body.

He especially liked George's height. With Tank being six seven, he didn't want to break his back bending down all the time. He loved the little mates the other warriors had at home, but he sometimes wondered how the hell they dealt with such short men.

So this was why Maverick insisted he return to the diner. He could have just come out and said the new cook was his mate. The Alpha didn't have to be all cloak and dagger about it.

Tank could feel the pull, his wolf wanting its mate. He had a feeling he was going to have a rough way going in convincing George that fate had chosen him to be Tank's.

Chapter Two

George looked back through the window to see Tank talking to the other two guys. Was he trying to add George to his harem of men? How many different men did he bring in here? George clenched his fists, angered that his body was betraying him. He had to admit at least to himself that Tank intrigued him. *Stupid libido.*

George slammed pots and pans around, angry that he was actually interested. What ticked him off the most was that with Tank's size, he had a feeling he would no longer be a top, and there was no way in hell he was bottoming for any man.

Never.

What did it matter? He wasn't going anywhere near Tank. He wasn't going to be run out of town or fight his way out of a mob of homophobes. He'd had enough of that to last this life and the next.

George grabbed the next order Kitty tossed up onto the window, trying his best to forget Tank Forney, which was pretty dang hard considering the feeling of wanting to rush out there and fall into the man's arms. George cursed as he slammed more things around.

"Everything okay in here?" Frank asked as he came out of his office.

"Yeah, just trying to get everything cooked," George replied.

"Let me know if it gets too much. I can always dive in and help."

"Nah, I can handle it." If he didn't stop throwing a fit, he would let on to everyone how he was feeling. That was something he'd rather keep to himself.

"Okay." Frank pushed past the double doors and walked off into the diner.

George slid back over to the window to get another peek. Tank was laughing with the two men at his table. George felt a twitch in his stomach at the gorgeous smile the guy had. It seemed to light up the entire room. He ducked down when Tank looked over his way. George scooted across the floor until he was no longer under the window then stood. Why was he acting like such a fool? Why did he care if the two men at his table were being graced by that heavenly smile?

He planted his hands on his hips as he exhaled. This was a clean break, not a romantic getaway. There could be no Tank in his life.

George's stupid brain wandered, daydreaming of a life where he didn't have to hide who he was. Did such a place even exist?

"Order up."

Startled, he came back to reality where he was standing in the middle of the kitchen he worked in and hiding who he was from the world. Rounding the island in the middle of the kitchen, he kicked his boot into the cabinet. It wasn't supposed to be hard here. His first day, and already he felt trapped. George shook his head. If Tank came at him again, he would just politely decline. There was no way he was risking anything again.

He remembered the look of pure pride his dad had when George's brother had announced he was going to be a daddy. His dad clapped Clyde's back and broke out the good bourbon. There was no way his dad would celebrate his other son announcing he was gay.

Trying to figure out why he liked men had kept him up numerous nights in his teenage years. He felt like he let everyone down.

George pushed the depressing thoughts away. There was nothing he could do about it. He was who he was whether he admitted to it or not.

Frank took him upstairs after the dinner rush had slowed to a crawl and the last of the customers were finishing up. The place was small. It had a tiny kitchenette, an open room that made up the dining room and living room. And a closet-size bedroom and a bathroom. It was perfect for George. After sharing a bunkhouse pretty much his entire adult life, having his own—as small as it was—was heaven.

George went back downstairs and gathered his belongings from the back of his truck. It wasn't much. Two suitcases and a duffel bag. Thankfully, the apartment upstairs was furnished.

He struggled to get the luggage up the narrow steps, tossing everything inside the door. He went back down to the diner to finish cleaning his kitchen. Frank stepped in, leaning against the industrial refrigerator. "So, what did you think of Tank?"

George didn't want to talk about the mountain of a man. He had never seen a guy that big in his entire life, and he was trying to forget him.

Frank wasn't helping.

"He's okay. A bit strange." George laughed nervously, uncomfortable with the topic. "Does he always grab people he just met?"

"Nope, just you." Frank watched him, probably trying to feel him out. Well, George wasn't spilling any of his beans.

"Well, I don't know what his problem is, but I'm not into men, so he can try and complete his harem somewhere else." George wiped the same spot repeatedly. It troubled him that he was feeling jealous of those men accompanying Tank. It just didn't make sense.

"That's not his harem. Those are his good friends' boyfriends. The guys earlier with him were just friends as well." George stopped momentarily then continued to wipe down. He didn't care if Tank was free game. He wasn't taking the bait. What the heck was with Frank anyway? Was he some sort of self-proclaimed matchmaker? His curiosity was piqued, though.

"There are gay men here?" George asked nonchalantly, as if it was just a curious question.

"Yep, a whole lot of 'em. Don't bother us town folk. They contribute a lot to the community, and they're nice fellas." Frank walked out of the kitchen, leaving George to sort out this new tidbit of information.

George absorbed what Frank had just revealed to him. Not only was the town accepting, but there were openly gay men who lived here? Even if he believed Frank, and he wasn't sure if he did just yet, Tank still wasn't his type. Those men weren't his harem. Just friends? Dammit, why did Frank have to open his piehole?

George cut the lights and dragged his tired bones upstairs, his mind in a whirl over the emotions assailing him. He thought of Jesse as he dropped down on the couch. His stomach tightened at the betrayal once more. George had loved the man, given his heart freely, and then he was crushed. He couldn't go through that again.

He dug through his duffel bag and pulled a few CDs out, opening the stereo's compact disc player up and tossing it in, and finding the song he was looking to hear. "To Make You Feel My Love" by Garth Brooks. He laid his head back against the couch, thinking of his lost love and broken heart. George quickly changed songs. He wasn't going to sit and wallow in self-pity. It was over, and he needed to move on. Leave Jesse in Wyoming and begin his new life.

His new, lonely life.

* * * *

Tank paced the halls of the Den. He wanted George. He wanted to hold him, claim him. His head hurt thinking of the possible ways to convince the cowboy that they were fated to be together. He pulled up the image of George's beautiful, crystal-blue eyes and his sandy-blond hair. The goatee was rugged, and Tank thought it added to the rough, manly look. He had a cute cowboy butt, too. A butt Tank was dying to sink into.

"Ugh." He couldn't take this. He wanted his mate. Why was he being so damn pigheaded? He should just go down there and demand that George come home with him. He would make the man see that he would love him unconditionally, treat him like a king.

"Yeah, right, and then get arrested," Tank mumbled.

"You know, it's a sign that you're losing it when you start talking to yourself." Cody walked up behind Tank.

"I'm not. Well, I am, but I'm so damn frustrated." Tank rubbed his hands over his head. Why was he torturing himself like this? How did the other warriors handle it when they were claiming their mates?

"What's got the giant in a tizzy?" Cody raised a brow.

"I found my mate, but he doesn't want anything to do with me." Tank leaned against the wall and stared up at the ceiling. Why did it have to be so complicated?

"Whoa. Who?" Cody asked in surprise. This irritated an already irritated man. Didn't anyone think he deserved to have a mate, or did they think he was only good enough to be a babysitter to theirs? Tank pushed the thought away. He knew he was just being cranky.

"George Knight." Tank said his name in reverence.

"Wait, my new cook?" Cody owned half the diner and had been a lousy cook for awhile until he and Frank found a replacement. The last one quit when business picked up so quickly. Tank would be forever grateful to the guy who quit. That is, if he ever convinced George they were mates.

"Yeah," Tank blew out.

"You do know why he came here, right?" Cody squatted down next to Tank who had slid down to the floor.

"No." He looked over at Cody, hopeful for an answer that may solve his problem.

"He's been kicked off of three ranches when they found out he was gay and had the love of his life crush his heart by denying him when it counted. He's bound to be scared to reveal his sexual preference."

"You think that's it? That's why he denied me?" Tank stood, hope flooding him.

"I'd say so, but don't quote me on it, buddy." Cody stood as well, clapping Tank on his back.

Tank watched Cody walk away. So he had to find a different approach for his mate. What? How do you convince a man that hid who he was to not hide it? Well, he was right about one thing, George was going to be a challenge.

* * * *

Tank woke the next morning, making a phone call before he left for the diner. He planned on eating three square meals there every day until his mate gave in.

He waited outside until Cody came and opened the place up.

"Anxious I see." Cody opened the door and let his mate, Keata, in first, then Tank.

"Tank have mate?" Keata asked as he hopped up on the stool at the counter. Keata was from Japan. He and his cousin Kyoshi had been kidnapped off the streets and smuggled across the ocean, only to get away and end up mating two of the Sentries. He was a dear friend of Tank's. The little guy could ask Tank for anything, and he would give it.

"Yeah, but mate don't want Tank." He sat next to the short mate.

"He will. You good catch." Keata beamed up at the warrior.

Cody growled. "Flirting with my mate, Tank?"

"He started it." Tank defended with a grin. Everyone knew that aside from their Commander, Hawk, who killed anyone who looked cross eyed at his mate, Johnny, Cody was head over heels for Keata and extremely protective of him, more so than the rest of the mated wolves. Cody and Hawk took protection to a whole new level. Keata had been kidnapped by the American who originally brought him over here, and Cody went nuts tearing up the video store they had been in, shifting in plain view searching for his mate, the Prince of vampires finally finding and returning Keata.

"Just chill, Tank. Don't come on too strong," Cody offered.

Tank took a deep breath then exhaled. "I won't." He was nervous as hell and excited at the prospect of seeing his mate again. His hands began to sweat and butterflies flapped their wings in his stomach. All the sudden, he felt like he was going to be sick. "I can't do this." Tank stood, but Keata pulled at his arm.

"Relax." Keata patted his arm.

"Yeah, okay. Relax." Tank sat back down.

"Morning, folks." George jogged down the steps from his apartment, and Tank shot off of his stool and out the front door.

* * * *

"He doesn't like people saying 'morning'?" George stared after Tank, wondering what he had said to upset the guy.

Cody stared openmouthed at the wind Tank left behind when he rushed out. "Guess not." Cody closed his mouth.

"Should I have said hello?" George eyed the door. He had decided last night that he would play things by ear, feel the town out, and maybe, just maybe, give Tank half a chance and see what happened. If they were really as gay-friendly as Frank claimed, then maybe he could have a chance at a real life here.

Guess he just found out what would happen.

"No morning person," a short man sitting at the counter defended Tank.

"Hi. Who are you?" George extended his hand only to have one of his two bosses growl at him. George shrugged Cody off and shook the little cutie's hand.

"Keata, Cody's mate." He smiled.

"Mate?" He looked from Keata to Cody.

"He's from England." Cody was obviously covering Keata's mistake. But the question was, what mistake?

"But he's Japanese." George scratched his head.

"Yeah, uh, migrated?" Cody quickly went to the office he shared with Frank, removing himself before he stuck his foot deeper into his mouth. George figured that much out, but what was he hiding?

"You really from England?" George asked Keata.

"I, uh, don't speak English." Keata ran after Cody.

Well, he seemed to know how to clear a room real quick. George looked once more at the door before he went into the kitchen to get things ready for the day.

* * * *

Tank sat on the steps to the post office, feeling like a real idiot.

"Stupid, stupid, stupid." He groaned.

George was actually speaking to him, and he ran out of there like a damn pup. Tank ran his hands over his head. He needed to get back in there, but would his mate still talk to him? Standing, he brushed off his bottom and walked back to the diner.

No one was around, so he took a seat at the booth. The morning rush started, and Kitty coming over to take his order. Tank ate slow, waiting for another chance to talk to George.

A delivery person came in with a bouquet of flowers, handing them over to Kitty.

"For me?" She smiled and smelled the yellow roses.

"No, ma'am, they're for a George Knight." The delivery man had her sign then left.

"George, you got some damn flowers," Kitty yelled to the back.

Tank wondered what her problem was. Was she jealous she didn't get any? He watched George come out and look around then take the card from the metal holder. He opened it then blushed, his eyes looking to Tank before darting away.

"Who's got the hots for you?" Kitty tried to look over George's shoulder.

"Stop." George shrugged her away, aware Tank was watching.

"I still think you should go out with me. I'll make it worth your while." She pinched George's ass cheek.

Tank growled. So that's why she acted jealous. She wanted his mate. Tank was going to have a talk with Cody about sexual harassment on the job.

George grabbed the vase and headed back into the kitchen, looking over his shoulder at Tank quickly before he smiled and disappeared.

Tank mentally air pumped his arm. Score one for Operation Win His Mate.

When Tank's plate came, it had extra helpings of hash browns and four eggs instead of two.

"Guess his mind is on those flowers. He gave you more than you ordered." Kitty sat his plate down.

Tank pulled his lip up in a sneer then caught it. He didn't want to out George if he wasn't ready for it.

"Hungry, big guy?" Kitty winked at him.

"Always." Tank pasted a smile on that he didn't feel. He was really beginning not to like her.

Chapter Three

George had just pulled his breakfast quiche from the oven, setting it on a cooling rack, when he heard the door swish open from the diner. He looked over to see Tank standing right inside the kitchen. George looked back down at the oven, not knowing what to say.

"Hi," Tank offered first.

"Uh, hi." George straightened, looking over to the counter to see who was watching. Kitty was over at a table taking orders, not paying any attention.

"No one saw me come in." Tank rubbed his hands on the front of his jeans. George was glad he wasn't the only one nervous as hell.

"You really shouldn't be in here." He regretted the words as soon as he said them. Tank's face fell.

"Okay, sorry to bother you." Tank turned to leave.

"Wait, I—I shut down around nine. Maybe we could hang out or something." George felt like he was sixteen all over again, fumbling over words, not sure what to say. He knew he said the right thing when Tank's dark brown eyes lit up.

"Okay. I'll be back then." Tank left with a big, goofy grin on his face.

George smiled. For a big guy, he sure was insecure. He liked that. It made Tank seem less intimidating.

He whistled his favorite country song as he worked around the kitchen the rest of the day, stopping occasionally to smell the beautiful flowers Tank had sent him. Time seemed to move slowly, maybe because he couldn't stop glancing at the wall clock.

"How ya hanging in there, George?"

"So far, so good. I hadn't anticipated such a crowd. When you said rush, I was expecting maybe half of what we get." George chuckled as he wiped the marble top island off.

"That's why the last cook quit. You sure you can handle it? I need to know. Before you came, Cody was cooking, and let me tell you, it was frightening." Frank shuddered.

"Nah, I can handle the folk. Took me a minute to get a routine, but it ain't so hard." George wrapped the raw chicken up that he'd been marinating for lunch and stored it in the refrigerator.

"Nice flowers." Frank quirked a brow and nodded over to George's vase of yellow roses.

All he could do was shrug. He wasn't about to explain anything especially when he was still trying to figure things out. "Thanks."

"I'll let you get back to work. Just wanted to check up on you and see how things were going."

George leaned his hip against the counter. What would Tank want to do tonight? The guy hadn't mentioned anything, and George wasn't familiar with the town. Frank may be claiming it was a gay-friendly town, but George in no way was ready to use public displays of affection in front of people. He wasn't even ready for the attention Tank was giving him.

When the clock read eight thirty, George closed the kitchen down and hit the lights. He ran up the stairs to get ready. He had thirty minutes until Tank showed up. That should be plenty of time to get his food encrusted clothes off and look presentable.

He kicked his boots off then hurriedly pulled his T-shirt above his head. Once the water was regulated, George pulled his jeans and underwear off, tossing his socks onto the pile. The shower took only moments. His nerves made him rush through everything.

George cursed when he tripped over his duffel bag. He needed to slow down. Pulling up from the floor, he made his way over to the dresser.

"What are you acting like this for?" he asked his reflection in the large mirror that hung there. Deciding he wasn't out to impress the big guy, George just grabbed a clean pair of jeans and a T-shirt from his bag. He really needed to unpack.

Ready to go, George grabbed his Stetson from off the hook and placed it on his head. Taking one last look in the mirror to make sure he looked presentable, he cut the lights and jogged down the steps.

* * * *

Tank paced behind the diner. It was only eight thirty. He knew he was early, but he'd been too excited to sit still. He showered and shaved, trying to look his best for his mate. The lights in the diner went off, and Tank's hands got sweaty just at the thought of finally spending some alone time with George. A half hour passed, and Tank got more agitated. Then, the back door pushed open.

He could see that George had showered and was wearing clean clothes. He looked absolutely stunning. His crystal-blue eyes were twinkling as he smiled at Tank. Damn, he actually had dimples. Tank had an urge to run his tongue along the indents. It took sheer willpower not to grab his mate into his arms and molest him right behind the dinner. It wouldn't help his cause either.

"Hi." George stepped out of the door and over to his right, looking at Tank from under his long, blond lashes.

"Hey. You, uh, wanna go for a walk?" Tank rubbed his hands down the front of his jeans again, his palms stayed wet around this guy.

"Okay." George stepped closer, and Tank noticed that George was the perfect height, the top of his head reaching Tank's shoulders.

"I hear you're from Wyoming. What's that like?" He walked George toward the town square, keeping a respectable distance. For now.

"Wide-open spaces and plenty of room to ride your horse." George sighed. "I do miss that. Miss the early morning rides I took with my horse, Daisy."

"I never rode a horse. Is it hard?"

"Nah, just gotta know how to handle 'em. They feel what you feel, so you have to be calm around them." George visibly relaxed. Tank wasn't making any moves on him. It was like two old friends taking a stroll. No pressure. Tank planned on keeping it that way until his mate became accustomed to him.

"Maybe one day you can teach me." They circled around the gazebo that sat in the middle of the park, strolling slowly, enjoying each other's company.

"Sure, I'd like that. It'll be nice to get back in the saddle. Can I ask you something?" George stopped and looked up at Tank.

"Okay."

"What did you mean yesterday when you grabbed me and said I was yours? What gives?"

The scene played in Tank's mind. He couldn't outright tell the man they were mates. He knew he would have to in the near future, but right now he just wanted to enjoy the time they were spending together without making it complicated. "Can I wait to answer that until we get better acquainted?" Until he had the guts to tell George about his wolf.

George studied him for a moment then nodded. "Promise you'll answer it though?"

"I promise. Can I ask you something now?" Tank shoved his hands in the front pocket of his jeans.

"Okay." Scratching the back of his neck, his mate looked like he wasn't sure he wanted to answer any personal questions.

"What's up with Kitty?"

A look of relief flooded George's face. "Is it that obvious?" George chuckled. "I think she's trying to make me a daddy."

"What?" Tank thundered out.

"Whoa, big fella. I said *trying*. She's got a dozen of them runnin' around at home. She doesn't think I know. I may be a hick, but I'm not that stupid." George laughed.

Tank could listen to his laugh for hours on end and never tire of it. "So, you're not interested in her?"

"Nah, ain't my type." They began to walk again, heading back toward the diner.

"What's your type?" *Please let him say me.*

"Not sure, but she ain't." Tank could tell he was hiding the fact that he was gay. Frank told him that he let his mate know how gay-friendly the town was. Well, most of the town. He remembered the scuffle the mates had in the bathroom of the diner a while back. Four cowboys from the local ranch seemed to have a problem with the sexual preference of others and wanted to make an example out of the mates. Boy, were they surprised when the mates defended themselves. Hell, Tank had been shocked.

They ended at the back entrance of the diner, Tank wishing they had taken a longer route. He didn't want to let George go. Dammit, why couldn't he just take him home and claim him? Tank wanted to stomp his foot like a five-year-old having a fit. It wasn't fair.

"Well, it was nice talking with ya. I guess I'll see you around the diner. And thanks for the roses." George turned to leave, but Tank wasn't having it. He pulled his mate into his arms, crushing his lips to the softest set he'd ever tasted. George moaned and leaned into Tank, battling for domination. Tank knocked George's Stetson off and grabbed a handful of blond hair, pulling his mate's head back and delving deeper.

George broke the kiss. "Tank."

Tank stopped the protest by kissing George again, his taste like a fresh summer morning rain. Tank got lost in the sweetness of his mate's mouth.

Tank could tell George wanted to push him away, but his mate surprised him by grabbing his face instead. Tank reached a hand around his mate's neck, pulling him closer. This must have been too much because George pushed him away, a look of mixed lust and confusion in his eyes.

"George." Tank reached out, but George stepped away.

"I can't, Tank. I just…can't." George pulled the door open and ran upstairs.

Tank stood there, stunned. What did he do wrong? Reaching down to grab George's hat, he dusted it off and inhaled the scent of his mate.

He had thought things were going well. George seemed like a really nice guy, a guy Tank wanted to get to know better. His heart reached out to the guy, wondering what it was like to deny who you truly were.

Never in his life had Tank thought to lie about being gay. Even when his pack turned their backs on him, he stood proud and tall, leaving them behind. To be kicked off of three ranches must have been devastating to the cowboy. Tank couldn't even imagine someone telling him to get out. He left his pack of his own free will.

He had an urge to drive to Wyoming and kick everyone's ass that offended his mate.

Staring up at the apartment, he was torn between just going home or knocking the door down and claiming what was his. He'd force George out of the closet. He shook his head, knowing he really wouldn't do that.

With a sigh, Tank started walking slowly back toward his truck.

* * * *

George paced his small apartment, thinking about the best kiss he had ever had. He felt at a loss being away from Tank, and that scared the shit out of him. George hit the on button to the stereo and blasted Faith Hill's "Free," letting the melody take him away.

The image of that big Clydesdale of a man made his groin ache. He couldn't seem to get his mind past that kiss. He'd never had one— or given one, for that matter—with such passion in it.

"Oh, man." George flopped down on the couch. "I'm hooked." He groaned loudly. He sat up when he remembered his hat downstairs. It was his favorite one, his only one at the moment. George slowly crept down the steps, listening for any sign that Tank still remained. When he heard nothing, he pushed the back door open. He looked down where it had dropped after that amazing kiss, but it was gone.

"Dammit," he bit out softly. He felt naked without it. It was all he had left from his mama, and he wanted it back. His mother had bought it for him on his eighteenth birthday, a year before she passed, and it brought him comfort. It made him feel closer to her, like he still had a part of her with him.

"Late for a human to be out."

George looked over his shoulder to see two men standing off in the shadows. *Human?* What the heck were these two talking about?

"He'd make a nice snack." One of them snickered.

"I don't know about that. My hide is pretty rough." George turned to face them, squaring his shoulders. He didn't run from anyone, least of all cowards who prayed on unsuspecting folk in the shadows.

"Doesn't matter. You'll do." They stepped forward, their fangs gleaming under the moonlight.

Fangs? What the hell was going on here?

George backed away, trying to make his way to the side of the building for more room to deal with these…whatevers.

"Don't run. It won't hurt…much."

George spun around and took off, rounding the corner of the diner and heading for his truck. He needed the rope that lay in the bed of it.

"I like a chase." One of them laughed with glee.

"Then come chase me, you no good cow patty." George skidded to a stop by his truck and swung his arm over the bed. Thank goodness he had left that piece of rope in there.

"What's going on, George?"

George turned his head to see Tank standing by his truck, his damn hat in the man's hand. He walked forward, stopping in front of the big galoot.

"What'd you do, wait until my back was turned and steal it?" George reached out and grabbed his hat from Tank's fingers.

"Now, wait one minute. You left it on the ground. I was going to return it in the morning," Tank defended himself.

"Likely story," George argued. He dusted the hat as if Tank's fingerprints were smudged all over it then set it atop his head.

"Who are they?"

George looked over his shoulder to see the two men round the corner and start their way slowly. He waved them off. "Hell if I know. Something about a snack" George turned back to Tank, ticked that the man was smirking. "That hat's special to me, I don't appreciate no one touchin' on it."

Tank waggled his finger in George's face. "I said I was gonna return it."

"Sure ya were." George smacked Tank's hand away from his face.

The two men showed their fangs, circling the arguing pair.

"George, get in my truck, I've got vampires to deal with." Tank shoved George at the passenger side of his pickup.

"I ain't no damn girl, I can defend myself against…vampires?" George spun around to look at the two men, who were getting closer, their teeth long and sharp and protruding from their mouths.

"Yeah, vampires. Now stop arguing, and get inside. I won't have my mate in harm's way." Tank once again pushed George to get in.

"Will you stop that?" George smacked Tank's hands. "I said I ain't a girl, and what's this mate crap I keep hearing about? I swear I'll hit you if you say something about England."

"Dammit, I'm a wolf, and you're my mate. I wanted to wait and tell you when I thought you could handle it." Tank put his hands on his hips, seeming exasperated that George was being so difficult. *Well, too dang bad.*

"Mate? What the hell does that mean?"

"It means I claim you, and then you belong to me." Tank

narrowed his eyes. "Are you going to argue with me about it?"

He glared at Tank, frowning. "Claim me? I ain't being claimed by no one, partner, least of all a Neanderthal like you." George pointed his finger up into Tank's face.

"George." Tank growled a warning.

"Don't George me." George swung around, connecting his fist into one of the vampire's jaw. Just because he was arguing didn't mean he wasn't paying attention to what the two were doing. The guy stumbled back, and that was all George needed. He swung again and again, not letting up. He saw he was having little effect on the guy, but he knew if he stopped, he'd be toast.

"Dammit, George. Get over here where I can protect you," Tank shouted to him in irritation.

"Don't." *Whack.* "Need." *Smack.* "Your." *Crunch.* "Protection." George knocked the guy on his ass. He looked over his shoulder briefly to see Tank had the other vampire by his throat, squeezing the undead life out of him.

"Watch out." Tank pointed to the one George was dealing with.

He turned around to see the guy had gotten back up. George reached into the bed of his truck and grabbed the rope, running down the sidewalk with it with the vampire close behind. He stopped, whirled the rope high in the air, and lassoed the sneaky fucker. George ran back and looped the rest of the rope around the guy, knowing it wasn't going to hold him for long.

George dragged the guy back over to Tank and tossed him on the ground. Turning to the mountain of a man, he thinned his lips. "I ain't being claimed, Tank."

"Why not? I'd be gentle. Don't let my size scare you." Tank softened his eyes on him.

"Gentle? You saying we got to have sex?" George laid his cowboy boot on the vampire's chest to stop him from getting up.

"Well, yeah. That's how I would claim you." Tank looked at him like it should have been obvious.

"I ain't no one's bottom boy. I top. That's what I do." George put his hands on his hips, blowing up a puff of air to knock away the bangs that had fallen into his eyes.

"Uh, guys. I'm not hungry anymore, so I'll just be on my way." The vampire lying on the ground tied up spoke.

"Shut up," George and Tank said in unison.

"Don't you think you need to call for backup? Ain't gonna hold him for long." George pointed behind him at his capture.

"Fine, but we're not finished with this conversation." Tank pulled out his cell phone and talked rapidly into it, sliding it back into his front pocket.

"Oh, we're done. Wolf or no wolf, claim or no claim, I ain't doin' it. You ain't toppin' me." George dropped down on the wiggling vampire and sat on his chest, and then he cocked his arm back and punched him in the face.

"What was that for?" the vamp yelled.

"Sit still." George pointed a finger at him in warning.

"Be reasonable, mate. How else am I supposed to claim you?" Tank walked over with the other vampire still in his hand.

"Guess I'll have to top you. Should work the same." He crossed his hands over his chest.

"No, it wouldn't. I have to be inside of you when I bite you." Tank threw his arms up in frustration, the guy lifting with his move.

"Why can't I bite you? Be inside of you?" George bit out.

"Duh, you have no canines, at least not long enough. Besides, I don't think it works that way."

George fell on his ass when the vampire broke the ropes and got to his feet.

"I ain't that damn hungry." He turned around and stormed off toward the woods. "Crazy-ass people around here, I swear..." he mumbled as he disappeared.

"Now see what you done did—"

"I did? You're the one being so damn difficult." Tank tossed his capture to the ground and stepped chest to chest with his mate.

"To hell with this." The second vampire got to his feet and took off after the first one.

"Me? You're the one who wants to fuck me. No way, no how." George stepped back, crossing his arms over his chest. Telling Tank in no uncertain terms that it wasn't happening.

Headlights flooded them, and three large guys got out of the truck with a look of bewilderment crossing their faces. They looked from Tank to George, their eyebrows furrowing.

"That way." Tank jammed his thumb over his shoulder, pointing in the direction the pair had taken off in.

The three nodded and ran, shifting as they entered the woods.

"Where the hell did I move to? Brothers Grimm? Wolves and vampires. Next you're gonna tell me trolls live under a damn bridge somewhere." George paced over to his truck, leaning against it, crossing his ankles. "Seems we're at an impasse, Tank. Sorry, I ain't bottoming."

Tank rubbed his hands over his head, looking like he was ready to punch someone out. Maybe the guy should have held onto the vamp a little longer and taken his frustrations out on him. Whatever the case may be, George wasn't budging.

"Okay, just once then. Long enough to claim you? We can argue over topping after that until the cows come home," Tank pleaded.

"No." George pushed off his truck, walking back to the rear of the diner.

"George," Tank called out to him.

"No," George shot over his shoulder as he disappeared.

"Fuck," Tank yelled in frustration, loud enough for George to hear him.

Chapter Four

"I'd like to invite you to dinner at my house." Tank stood inside the kitchen, watching George cook. Man, if he wasn't a gorgeous sight. Tight denim jeans, midnight-blue T-shirt stretched over an impressive chest, and black cowboy boots to top it off. Tank fought the urge to toss his mate over the marble countertop and fuck his brains out.

"Okay. You do know I don't get off until nine?" George turned around and stared at Tank, his blue eyes twinkling in the light.

Tank wanted to lick the goatee around his mouth and nip at the soul patch under his bottom lip. "Yeah. Pick you up then?"

"I can drive. Just give me your address. Shouldn't be too hard to find." George spoke softly, and Tank's hard-on throbbed in his jeans. His mate looked like one of those boy-next-door types. Handsome, rugged, and drool-worthy.

"Okay, I'll go write it down." Tank pushed the kitchen doors open and headed back into the dining area. He reached under the counter for a scrap sheet of paper, borrowing a pen from the cup filled with them by the register.

"Got a date?" Cody asked quietly as he walked next to Tank

"Yeah, he's agreed to come to dinner. What do I feed someone who can cook when I can't?" Tank scribbled down the address and the directions. It was an estate buried far back from the country road, set back into the forest for privacy and room for the wolves to run and be themselves.

"Takeout?" Cody suggested.

"Never thought of that. Maybe I can get two to-go orders."

"Tank, I wouldn't suggest having him cook what he's gonna come over and eat. Try the Chinese place in town. I hear they're pretty good." Cody chuckled.

"Right. Never thought of that."

"Tank have mate?" Keata asked from the stool by the register.

"Almost, little buddy. Almost." Tank ruffled Keata's hair as he stepped back in the kitchen and gave George the directions, both men staring at one another for a moment. Tank knew George felt the pull, and that's why he kept agreeing to see him. Now he just needed him to agree to the claiming, which was easier said than done.

* * * *

George checked the paper Tank had given him then looked back up at the massive house he was sitting in front of. This couldn't be right. The place was huge. There were at least ten pickups lining the gravel drive and three large SUVs. Did Tank have a party going on in there?

George cut the engine and opened his door. He stood there for a moment wondering if he had the right address. He spotted Tank's half-ton truck and knew he was in the right place. Taking a deep breath, he climbed the steps and rang the doorbell. He wasn't much of a party person. Maybe he could make an excuse and get out of there.

"Can I help you?" A small man answered the door. He looked like his boss's mate, Keata.

"I'm here to see Tank." George stepped back when a large man growled and grabbed the smaller man into his arms.

"Haven't I told you about answering the door, dragonfly?"

George noticed the guy's eyes swirled with different colors. It was hypnotizing. The little man laughed and kissed the larger man, hugging him close. A part of George envied the love they obviously had for one another. He wanted something like that for himself.

And to be so open with it? That was a pipe dream for George.

"He's here to see Tank." The little guy wrapped himself around the larger one.

"Come on in. You must be George. I'm Storm." Storm stuck his hand out and shook George's. "And this little man is my mate, Kyoshi."

"He looks like Keata." George stepped into the foyer, noise assailing him immediately. He heard whooping and loud rock music that threatened to burst his eardrums.

"You know my cousin?" Kyoshi beamed.

George's nerves were beginning to fray with that heavy metal music. He was expecting to see kids run out of there with the loud video game noise. "Yeah, I work at the diner. He's there a lot with Cody." He glanced at the room with noise again. Maybe he should have popped a few aspirin before he got here.

"You must be the new cook Frank hired." Storm led him to a room any man would be envious of, except for the loud music. There were two suede couches to the left with a poker table behind it, and four short men sat at it playing poker with...pretzels? They were using pretzels instead of poker chips. He looked off to the right and saw a large billiard table with two large men playing a game and a full bar to the left of that. A dartboard hung on the wall close to the pool table.

George looked over when he heard yelling. In front of the couches was a large flat-screen television, and two men were jumping around, shouting curses at each other while playing a video game. George wished he could find the mute button and turn the damn music off. His headache was getting worse from it.

A small man ran up to him, his golden curls bouncing as he ran, "I'm Johnny. You must be George, Tank's mate." He hugged George.

George stood there stunned, the little appendage hanging on to him for a brief moment before letting go. A growl ripped through the air, and George's head snapped up to see the fiercest man that he imagined could be a person's worst nightmare. The kind of man you crossed the street to avoid. He had blue-black hair and stood as tall as Tank, except this guy looked like he just walked out of the bowels of hell.

"Sorry, Johnny gets a little excited." The man turned around and picked the little blond up. "What have we talked about, pretty baby?"

Pretty baby? George's head was spinning. Maybe this wasn't such a good idea. He felt out of place. It was like little guys versus big guy in this place, and George was in between. Well, not all the guy's were short. Two of the guys sitting off in a corner looked to stand just a tad shorter than George. They were sitting at the poker table, and they also looked similar to one another. They must be related. One had piercings decorating his ears and bottom lip. The other had hair all the way to his waist in a raven-black color.

"You made it."

George turned around to see Tank standing behind him, smiling. Tank looked amazing. George had no clue he could be turned on as much as he was by black fatigues and a black T-shirt that had to be a size triple X. The damn shirt stretched across a chest so full of muscles that George wanted to lick his lips.

Tank wasn't even his type, but George knew a hot guy when he saw one, and he was looking right at one. He swung his head around when he heard clatter over by the pool table. Two large men were standing chest to chest with each other, the man with black-and-blond hair was snarling.

"Don't pay any attention to Murdock and Gunnar. They're just competitive." Tank chuckled. "They're harmless."

"Yeah, they really look harmless." The one with the black and blond hair stood a few inches taller than George. He looked like he was a world-champion weight lifter with all the muscles he sported.

The other one was George's height and with the same blond hair he had, only this guy was more firm, not bulky. George thought he was insane for challenging the other guy.

"Come on, let's eat." Tank led him down a hallway that seemed to have a thousand doors. George noticed mahogany double doors that were open revealing an expansive library. These guys must be loaded. He felt slightly intimidated by that. He was just a poor country boy trying to get by, and here these guys were living it up. He wasn't jealous of their wealth. It was just overwhelming. As a poor farm boy, he wasn't used to such luxuries.

"I was going to have us eat in the formal dining room, but it seemed a little impersonal. I hope you don't mind the kitchen." Tank led him into a large open kitchen with a breakfast table that sat eight. The kitchen had green marble countertops and a chrome side-by-side refrigerator. It was beautiful. He smiled to himself when he saw that Tank had set the lighting low and had candles burning in a romantic setting.

Tank pulled his chair back, waiting for him to take it.

"I told ya I ain't a girl." George scoffed, crossing his arms over his chest.

"Humor me for tonight. Please?" Tank reached out and traced his fingers down George's forearm, causing him to get gooseflesh.

"Fine, but if you stand when I do, there's gonna be trouble." George heaved a sigh and allowed Tank to scoot his chair in.

Tank walked around to his side and began serving what looked like sweet-and-sour chicken. Did Tank cook this, or did he order it? George bit the inside of his mouth to stop the smile. He knew Tank had worked hard at this, and he wasn't going to complain or laugh at him. He appreciated the effort the man had gone through to impress him.

"I hope you like Chinese. I never thought to ask." He poured the red sauce over George's chicken, his hands shaking slightly.

"That's good." George put his hand up when Tank tried to add more chicken to his plate. "Thank you."

Tank smiled and sat back down, looking at George's plate and then back at his. He scooped a small amount of rice and chicken onto his plate.

George pointed his fork at Tank's plate. "I know you eat more than that. Don't stand on ceremony on my account. Eat up." George took a bite to cover his smile.

Tank tossed the fork down and grabbed the bite-size chicken with his fingers. He glanced up at George and chuckled as he placed another nugget in his mouth. Tank was trying really hard for him.

Tank gulped.

"You okay?" George set his fork down, staring at Tank with concern.

"Yeah, you're...just so breathtaking."

Did the big fella actually just blush? George's defensives lowered at the sight of this big galoot being so unsure and nervous. It made him feel ten feet tall, powerful, knowing he was the cause of Tank's vulnerability.

"Thanks." He shoved another forkful in his mouth, not sure what else to say. What do you say to something like that? Thank you seemed inadequate.

They finished their dinner. George helped Tank clean up while Tank protested that his guest shouldn't be cleaning. George scraped his plate and grinned at the take-out boxes he spotted in the trash. Maybe he would invite Tank to his place and cook him a nice, thick steak.

"Found me out."

George looked over his shoulder to see Tank standing so close behind him that he felt his breath on the nape of his neck.

"I had my suspicions. It was good anyway." George turned around and, closed the distance, taking Tank's lips in an unsure kiss. Tank didn't rush it this time. He kissed him back leisurely, as if sitting on a porch on lazy Sunday morning drinking lemonade. Tank's slow movements were setting George's blood on fire.

A tingle of excitement raced through George as Tank's fingers trailed up his arms. He could feel his body responding to that gentle touch, and George was frightened of this reaction, but he couldn't push the big teddy bear away.

Tank's slow, drugging kisses were taking him to another plane.

George caught the whimper before it could escape when Tank pulled back. His lips were still warm and moist from Tank's kiss.

They both stood there for a moment, as if coming out of a trance.

"Follow me," Tank said hoarsely, grabbing George's hand and leading him down the hall and through a door.

George dug his heels in when he saw that it was a bedroom. The bed that was in the center of the room could fit three Tanks in it. He admitted that the kiss was spectacular on a mega million dollar scale, but he wasn't sure about no dang bed.

"I thought we agreed we were at an impasse." George pulled his hand from Tank's, crossing his arms over his chest. He was irritated even further when he felt his body slightly shake.

"You agreed. No pressure. Just sit and talk with me." Tank crossed the room and sat on the edge of the bed, patting the space next to him.

George arched a brow. "Ain't that a line you use on an unsuspecting girl?"

"Don't know. Never been with one." Tank gave him a mischievous grin. George swam in a sea of insecurities. His body was pleading with him to go to Tank, but his mind and heart feared what could happen if he opened himself up. Being with a man larger than him, a man who didn't hide his sexual preference, was new to him, and George wasn't so sure he could handle it.

"Fine, but don't make me smack you." George stomped over to Tank and plopped down on the bed. Once again he crossed his arms to hide the shaking his hands were going through.

Tank pulled George's arm away from his chest and ran his fingers over the back of George's hand. The giant cleared his throat. "I'm a Timber wolf, two hundred and sixteen years old, and I've been looking for my mate since I was eighteen. That's you, if you haven't figured that out." Tank smiled softly at George. "We only get one.

One mate to last us till we reach one thousand years old. If you deny me, I have another seven hundred and eighty-four years to be alone."

"I thought you said no pressure." His head was in a whirl. This was all too much for him to take in. That's a long time to be alone. A wolf? One thousand years? Crap, he needed time to absorb this. "So if I let you claim me, I live that long, too?"

"Yes. You'll never get sick, you'll heal faster than an unmated human, and I *promise* to always make you happy and take care of all your wants and needs." Tank kept his head down, afraid of being rejected again would be George's guess.

"We still need to settle this bottom thing." Damn, what should he do? He didn't need Tank to take care of him, but to have that kind of devotion? His heart was torn.

"Just once? Let me claim you, George. That's all I ask. We can work anything out after that." Tank pleaded with his eyes.

George took of his hat, placing it beside him as he ran his hand through his hair. "Once?" He looked over to Tank, unsure of what he was about to agree to.

* * * *

"Promise." Tank's excitement was hard to contain. Was he really about to claim his mate? Would George agree to it? He held his breath as he waited for George's reply.

"How do we do this?"

Fuck yeah! He felt as though he'd just hit the lottery. Tank pulled George into his arms, laying him gently down on his back. "Just let me love you." Tank crawled over George. "Just once." His body trembled, and his hands shook as he feathered his fingers over the cowboy's tanned face.

George nodded and pulled Tank down for a scorching kiss. George wrapped his legs around Tank's waist and opened his mouth for Tank's exploration. As good as this was, Tank didn't want to waste time. The fear of his mate changing his mind had him moving away from the kiss.

Tank pulled back and unwrapped his mate's legs, pulling his T-shirt over his head and disrobing the rest of his clothes. He really didn't want to rush things, but his stomach knotted thinking of the man changing his mind at the last second.

George's eyes widened. "Is that a side of beef hanging between your legs? Oh, *hell* no. I think I may have changed my mind." George gulped audibly while staring at Tank's cock.

"Don't. Please. I won't hurt you," Tank pleaded as he reached down and pulled George to his feet, kissing his neck as he unsnapped his jeans, fishing his cock out and dropping to his knees.

"Tank," George croaked out as he pulled his shirt from over his head. Tank looked up into his mate's eyes, seeing the hesitation, fear, and lust burning in them. What had George been through to become so terrified of giving himself over?

"Just once," Tank whispered as he swallowed his mate's cock.

"Oh, fuck." George's head fell forward, grabbing Tank's shoulders as he swung his hips back and forth. Tank growled and applied suction, fucking his mouth on George's cock.

"Tank." George moaned. It sounded like an angel spreading its wings to Tank's ears.

His tongue danced with George's cock in a duel of seduction. Tank was now hopelessly addicted.

The coiled tension in his gut was too much, and Tank needed to claim what fate had given him while George was in agreement.

His mate cried out when Tank released him. That sound was like a symphony on a warm summer's night. "Strip," Tank commanded, and George didn't hesitate. He tossed his clothes off of his lean and— fuck, it was gorgeous—body, and crawled up on the bed, then lay on his back and grabbed his hardened shaft. Tank's body hummed at the sight before him.

"You gonna finish?" George smiled, and Tank lost the ability to breathe.

"Your smile must bring out the sun every morning." His mate's skin flushed, and there was never a more beautiful sight in heaven or on earth.

Tank smiled and crawled between George's legs, lowering as he took the cock down his throat.

"Yes, Tank." George hitched his hips, grabbing Tank's head as he pumped rapidly into Tank's mouth.

Tank wet a finger then pushed gently into his mate's ass. Knowing this was the first time the cowboy was being breached, Tank let his finger rest while he squeezed George's shaft. He ran his tongue up the length of George's shaft then crooked his finger

"Holy fuck!" George shot down Tank's throat, his back arching off of the bed. He drank his fill of his mate's seed until George had no more to give.

Tank didn't stop. He licked and sucked his way down until he lapped at his mate's balls, inhaling the strong scent of pure man between George's legs.

"I don't think I can survive until sundown if you do that again." George panted out.

"Like that?" Tank grinned around his mate's balls, sliding a third finger in.

"Whoa. If you hadn't noticed, your fingers are the size of sausages. Easy, boy." George moved a little to the side. Tank was afraid his cowboy was feeling a bit full and uncomfortable. "Relax, it gets better. Promise." Tank once again found George's prostate and slid his finger across, his mate hissing and bucking his hips. Tank leaned back and lubed his cock, impatient to claim what was his. "Ready?"

"No." George grabbed the sheets, turning his face away from Tank. The shame on the man's face tore Tank's mind in two. He wanted this cowboy more than tides needed the moons pull, but he didn't want to take if it wasn't being freely offered.

"George, look at me." Tank gently tugged his mate's chin until he was staring into those beautiful, crystal-blue eyes. "Just once."

George locked his jaw and nodded.

Tank pushed slowly past the ring of muscles, stopping when the head opened George wide. He gripped his mate's hips and pushed further, watching George's eyes for any sign of pain. If he asked, he would stop, although it would kill Tank now that he knew what an angel felt like.

Tank bottomed out and waited a moment until George's body adjusted to his invasion. This was the guy's first time on the receiving end, and Tank would do everything possible to make it pleasurable.

Tank wrapped George's legs around his waist, ghosting his hands down George's legs to ease the tension. He pulled back and then stroked long and deep. George's eyes closed, and his head fell back, his lips parting. He moaned as he bowed his back, taking Tank to a new depth.

"Do you accept me as your mate, George?" Tank's canines dropped, and his eyes shifted. He was terrified his mate would change his mind and leave now that he could see his wolf. What would he do if George decided not to go through with this?

"What am I supposed to say?" George groaned.

"A simple 'yes, Tank.'"

"Yes, Tank."

Tank was flying high. George had agreed to the claiming. He dropped to his forearms, licking a long path along the throbbing vein in his mate's neck before he struck.

Tank felt the ribbons of their souls unwind from each of them and entwine together, their heartbeats synchronizing. They were mated now. Tank was elated.

George shouted as Tank unloaded at the same time. His brain was in a fog of lust. Tank thrust harder, wanting his seed deep inside his mate. George's body was an addiction Tank knew he would never get enough of. Tank licked the wound closed as he panted for air. He fell to his side, reaching for his mate.

George threw his arm over his eyes and a short breath left his lips. He shook his head back and forth as if a battle was raging inside of him. Tank pulled his arms back and waited.

George rolled over and stood, grabbing his clothes.

"George, what's wrong?" Tank jumped up from his bed and tried to pull his cowboy into his arms. George pushed him back.

"I need time, Tank. This is a lot to wrap my head around. Please, just give me time." George's voice broke. He dropped his eyes and quickly dressed, never looking at Tank. "Can you please take me to my truck?"

Tank's heart was being ripped from his chest, but he nodded and got dressed. This couldn't be happening. He was finding it hard to breathe. His chest felt like the world was pressing against it and crushing it.

He had rushed his mate, and now he was paying the consequences. Tank held his feelings in, not showing how devastated and angry he was.

* * * *

George climbed into his truck and drove away, his heart hurting more the further from Tank he got. He needed time to himself to let his mind adjust to the fact that he was just fucked. He was just claimed. The feeling of being less than a man was strong. George was a rough and tough cowboy, but he felt like Tank's bitch.

He punched the dashboard, cursing because he wanted to turn his truck around and run into Tank's arms. Well, the guy got what he wanted. He claimed him, and now he could leave George the hell alone.

Chapter Five

Tank dropped onto the side of his bed, looking over at the rumpled sheets where moments ago he had held his mate. He dropped his face in his hands at the cruelty of fate. All he had wanted was what he saw in the other relationships in the house. He wanted those intimate moments, shared secrets, giggles.

Now he was left with a hollow hole that used to have his heart there. Tank clenched his fists as he stood. He wouldn't let George get away. He'd give him time to adjust, but he wasn't giving up. George was his, and nothing on earth would come between them, not even his own mate.

Tank rubbed his hands over his head as he wandered to the kitchen. He needed to think. He stood at the entrance to the kitchen, remembering the intimate dinner they shared. Tank had thought it was going so well. What had he done wrong that ran his cowboy away?

"No sad." Keata hugged Tank around the waist.

"Hey, buddy." Tank squeezed Keata then walked over to the refrigerator, eating his sorrows away.

"That bad?"

Tank looked over his shoulders to see the other mates entering the kitchen. He grabbed the leftover take-out container, wanting to go to his room to be alone. After what just happened, company was not something he wanted.

"So, we have a runaway mate on our hands?" Cecil took a seat at the table.

Tank just shrugged. He really didn't feel like talking about it.

"You know what you need, Tank?" Drew patted Tank on his back, unable to reach his shoulders.

Tank arched a brow and looked around the kitchen, not liking the looks in the little mates' eyes. They were up to something, but he just didn't know what...yet.

"You need intervention." Blair leaned against the counter.

"Intervention?" If Cecil cooked up this plan, Tank wasn't going to like it.

"Yep." Johnny piped up. "You need us." He pointed to every mate in the room.

"And how do I need you guys?" This should be good.

"You need us to show George what it means to be a mate." Oliver gave him an evil grin.

"Oh, no, stay away from him, Cecil," Tank warned.

"What?" Cecil asked innocently.

"Whatever you're planning, don't. He's skittish enough without you guys getting him landed in jail or something worse." Tank set his food down and glared at the mates. "I mean it. Stay away from him." Tank grabbed the white containers and stormed off.

* * * *

"Do we leave him alone?" Cecil asked the other mates.

"No, no!" Keata cheered as he threw his arms in the air.

"Didn't think so."

"So then what's your plan?" Oliver asked.

"I think I'll have one of the warriors take me to the diner and then slip into the kitchen. If he's mated to Tank, he can't be that difficult, right?"

"I don't know. He ran out of here pretty fast." Blair rubbed his jaw.

"You know the warriors will forgive us." Johnny giggled. "We all have a way of making them forget they're angry."

"You got that right." Oliver chuckled. "Although I don't want to push Micah too far. Those lectures make me want to pull my hair out."

No matter how the warriors reacted or how far the cowboy ran, Cecil would get to George one way or another.

* * * *

George threw another plate up onto the counter, mad at the fact that Tank hadn't shown up this morning. So what was he, a one-night stand? Was he only good for a roll in the hay, and then it was on to the next claiming? Did Tank even tell him the truth about the claiming? Was he just used and tossed aside?

George slammed the pots and pans. He was angry that he had given away his manhood only to be tossed aside like yesterday's trash.

He felt used.

"Hey."

George spun around to see one of the guys from Tank's house standing in the kitchen. He stood back, waiting to see what the little guy wanted.

"I'm Cecil."

"Nice to meet you, Cecil." George shook his hand, eyeing him warily.

"I got a proposition for you." Cecil leaned against the counter, watching George.

"And what might that be?" *Oh hell, look at that evil ass grin the man was sporting.* George had an urge to find holy water and dump it on this guy's head.

"You see, us mates can't go anywhere without a warrior tagging along. This whole vampire and rogue wolf thing..." Cecil spun his hands in the air. "I was thinking, since you're tall enough, and from the looks of you, strong enough, that maybe you could be our escort."

George didn't trust this guy. He had a gleam in his eye that he had seen bulls have right before they charged. He had to admit, though, he was intrigued. "So what are you proposing?"

"We want to go to a strip club." Cecil gave him an innocent smile. Like a snake right before he bit you.

"Is that right? And why would I take you guys there?" George was really starting to like this little guy. He had spunk. Maybe he had Cecil all wrong.

"'Cause you're nice, and 'cause we're going crazy sitting in the house, and the warriors would never in a million years take us. Please." He gave the best puppy dog eyes George had ever seen.

"I don't know. Wouldn't your *warriors* try and skin me alive for taking you?" George wasn't into pain. He could hold his own with the best of them, but taking on those giants would be suicide.

"No, you're a mate. They wouldn't touch you. Yell, maybe." Cecil clasped his hands together in a prayer, pleading with George.

"To hell with it. When do you want to go?" He'd never really had friends before. Being in the closet made him keep a distance from people for fear of them finding out. It was a new feeling, and he liked it.

"Yes! Thanks, G. How about tonight? We can sneak out the side entrance. There's a male strip club in the city, and we'll all pair up so were safe. Being on lockdown sucks." Cecil danced around.

"All right. I'll meet you at the side entrance at ten. I ain't waitin' around, so if you guys aren't there, tumbleweeds will be rolling behind me."

"Uh, okay. Whatever that means, we'll be there. You don't be late either. We have to be quick about it." Cecil held up his fist, George just staring at it.

"Like this." Cecil grabbed George's hand. "Make a fist." George curled his fingers in, and Cecil tapped theirs together.

"What does that mean? I ain't joinin' no damn gang." George grabbed his hand back.

Cecil fell over the counter, laughing. "No, silly, it means we agree. Or hello."

George eyed him curiously for a moment. "Ten. No later."

"You got it. Now I have to get back out there before the warriors come hunt me down." Cecil winked at him with that gleam still present and walked out of George's kitchen.

He seemed to be agreeing to a lot of crazy shit lately.

* * * *

George pulled his pickup to the side entrance, and all seven men dove into the cab as George sped off. He had an extended cab, so the shorter men were sitting on the larger ones' laps.

"We did it!" Johnny laughed as he high-fived Keata.

"What the hell did you guys get me into?" George steered the truck onto the highway, hightailing it out of there before he had a pack of wolves on his ass, trying to chew his tires off and eating him for a snack.

George pulled into the lot, everyone piling out like clowns coming out of a clown car.

"Everyone get a partner," Blair yelled over the excited chatter.

Drew grabbed George's hand. "Hi, I'm Drew. My mate is Remi." He smiled shyly at George.

"Hi, Drew." George tugged on Drew's hand as they made their way into the club. Cecil pulled them all to the front row, yelling out catcalls as the first stripper danced to his number.

"You guys really don't care who knows you're gay?" George looked down at Drew. His head was puzzled by this.

"Nope, as long as we have our mates, the rest of the world can suck weenies." Drew threw his head back laughing. "Get it?"

George chuckled. "I got it."

"Hey, G, get over here," Oliver yelled from across the room.

George led Drew over, and the mates pushed George up onto the stage. He stumbled up, tripping but righting himself. He was surprised and unsure of how to handle this.

"What the hell are you guys doing?" He tried to climb down, but the mates blocked him. Taking a step left or right didn't help, they just moved their bodies along with his, blocking his escape.

"Have a little fun," Kyoshi yelled up at him while laughing.

George spun around when hands grabbed his hips. A male stripper was winking at him. He leaned forward and whispered in George's ear. "They paid for me to dance with you. Just go with it."

George shot a glare at the mates as he stood still, not sure what he should do. The stripper began to dance around George, shimmying up and down George's back. The male dancer removed his top and tossed it aside, grabbing George's hips once again. "Loosen up." The guy grinned.

George looked back at the mates. They all had their wide eyes on him, waiting for him to have fun.

Fuck it.

George started wiggling his hips as the guy stripped his pants off. Nothing but a G-string on now. He tossed them aside and shimmied his ass so quickly George thought it looked like a bowl of Jell-O come to life.

"Go George, go George, go George." The mates were chanting as Johnny and Keata did the robot, bumping into one another and laughing.

George got into the spirit of things, and he sashayed his hips as he strut across the stage. Even the stripper stepped aside, enjoying George's performance.

He struck one hip out and slid his hand down the front of his shirt in a slow and suggestive manner. His eyebrow quirked, giving the mates his sexiest look.

They cheered and chanted, tossing bills at George. He was shocked to admit it, but he was having some dang fun up here.

* * * *

"Your damn mate is at it again!" The mated warriors stormed Maverick's office, their arms crossed over their chests, glaring at their Alpha.

Maverick pinched the bridge of his nose. Cecil was going to get him impeached. "Track them with the GPS."

"Can't, all the vehicles are accounted for and every room has been checked," Hawk bit out.

"Then how the hell did they get away?" Maverick's head fell back as he stared at the ceiling. It really needed to be dusted.

"George." Maverick said the word with confidence.

"Can't be. He doesn't want anything to do with me right now," Tank embarrassingly admitted.

"Call him Go there. I bet he isn't home and his truck is gone." Maverick stared Tank in his eyes, demanding he do it.

"If you say so." Tank pulled out his phone and called his cowboy.

* * * *

"Thanks." George panted as he jumped off the stage. "I had a good time."

Cecil noticed how he said it as though he were shocked.

"You know George, we're all mates, and we're all men. Just because we allow our mates to take us doesn't mean we're girls or anything. They love us and would give their lives for us, same as we would do for them." Cecil slid George an orange soda.

George eyed the glass. "I was driving so I guess I have to drink it, although a cold beer would hit the spot right about now."

Cecil smirked and sat back.

"When you hide it all your life, it's kinda hard to let that go. I want to be with Tank, just… hell, I don't know." George downed the soda, wishing it was hard liquor.

"He's a good guy with a kind heart, always looking out for us mates. Always nice. You couldn't do any better." Cecil hoped he was getting through because he really liked George and would love to have him as part of their makeshift family.

"You gave me a lot to think about. He is sweet." George blushed. "Cecil!"

Cecil's head snapped up. Oh shit, his mate sounded pissed.

"Where's my Keata?" Cody ran to Keata, pulling him into his arms as Hawk grabbed Johnny, peppering kisses all over his face.

"Relax, G got us. He wouldn't let anything happen to us, right?" Cecil turned toward George and saw the seat was empty. Traitor.

"Can we stay?" Blair asked his mate.

"If that's what you want, Sunshine." Kota looked over his shoulder. "What do you say, Maverick? Have a little fun *with* our mates?"

Maverick eyed Cecil, never able to stay mad at him for more than two seconds. "Okay, but no touching, or I'll have to kill some strippers."

* * * *

George slid next to Tank, staring at the stage as he pushed his fingers into Tank's hand.

Tank swallowed hard, not sure how to handle this. Did he pull his mate in his arms or let him make the moves? He decided to let George lead the way.

The warriors laughed as the mates whooped and hollered, crumbling the dollar bills up and tossing them on stage since they couldn't put it in their G-strings.

Cecil leaned forward, and Maverick growled, pulling his mate back. "Cecil," Maverick warned.

"What?" He looked at Maverick innocently.

"Having a good time?" Tank asked George, as he laughed at Cecil's antics.

"Yeah, I am." George leaned over and kissed Tank. Not a peck, but a full-blown, blazing kiss. He knew his cowboy was a little nervous doing it in public—a lot of nervous, if his stiffness was anything to go by. Tank took the kiss deeper until his mate laughed. Kind of an odd time to do that.

"What's so funny?" Tank pulled George closer, wanting another taste. Those kiss swollen lips called to him.

"Drew."

"You'll have to tell me about it sometime." Tank placed the pad of his index finger under his mate's chin, raising it, and kissed George again. "Will you stay the night with me?" He prayed he hadn't stepped over an invisible line and pushed too fast again.

"Okay."

Tank wanted to grab his cowboy and run home. Instead, he sat back and enjoyed watching the little guys jump around and toss money at the performers. He wrapped his arm around his mate, thankful Cecil and the others didn't listen to him when he warned them away from George.

Chapter Six

"I want to top this time."

Tank looked at George like he was the devil asking to barter his soul.

George waited for Tank to answer him, already feeling the animosity building inside of him. He knew Tank had never bottomed, but neither had he. He wasn't saying he didn't like it. It was different, and it had felt great, but it was his turn, dammit.

Tank nodded.

George wanted to chuckle. The man looked like he just agreed to go in front of a firing squad.

Tank must have thought he was sinking into George, please. Wait a minute, did Tank agree? "Really?" George stared at him openmouthed.

"Close your damn mouth, and I mean that literally. Nobody better find out." Tank grabbed the lube from the drawer, slapping it into George's hand.

They both fell over trying to get out of their clothes. George moved out of the way as Tank became unbalanced, tangled in his jeans, and nearly falling into him. The big galoot was too massive to catch. George would be scraping himself off of the wall.

"Swear." George grinned from ear to ear as he climbed onto the bed with Tank. "Okay, *mate*, bend over."

"Don't start, George." Tank growled as he climbed onto the bed, rolled over onto his back and spreading his legs.

"A guy's gotta have some fun..." He slapped Tank's hip. "Bend over."

"No." Tank crossed his arms over his chest.

"Why are you being so difficult? I gave it up without an argument. Now hush and roll over onto your damn knees." George slapped the lube bottle on Tank's thigh.

"Why can't we do it this way? I want to look into your eyes." Tank pouted. George thought he looked cute as a button with his bottom lip stuck out.

"That's so sweet…bend over." George narrowed his eyes on Tank.

"Fine, but I get to top you next." Tank rolled over to his knees.

"Good lord."

"What?" Tank looked over his shoulder.

"Just, uh, wow." George lubed his hand, spearing two fingers into Tank's tight hole.

"Hey, I may be a big guy, but that's virgin territory down there." Tank grunted.

"Sorry, got a little excited." George began a scissor-like motion with his fingers, reaching his other hand down to cup Tank's sac.

"More." Tank moaned.

"Thought you'd like it." George wiggled his fingers around, trying to find that sweet spot of Tank's.

"What's that suppose to mean?"

"Will you stop arguing? You're killing my hard-on." George crooked his fingers again.

"Holy fuck!"

Found it.

"Feels good, don't it?" George speared a third finger in, stretching his mate the best he could. "Ready?"

"No."

"Slidin' my snake in your hole anyway." George slapped his ass. "Cowboy up."

"Huh?"

"Here comes the weasel." George pushed in, stopping when Tank stiffened. Fuck, he was tight. He had to close his eyes and take long, slow breathes to calm his impending orgasm. His eyes slowly opened when Tank tapped him on his hip.

"Okay." Tank pushed back a little as George eased forward.

"Tank, fuck, so tight." George barely held it together with the enjoyment of feeling such a hot, tight ass wrapped around his cock.

"No talking." Tank moaned.

"Why?"

"I don't know. Hush." Tank pushed back.

"Why?"

"George," he warned.

"Why?" George began to laugh. He sounded like a five-year-old, but he was having fun for the first time during sex, and he liked it. Tank was something he never expected, and surprisingly was beginning to see that he couldn't live without.

Tank began laughing with him. "Just fuck me already. And if you say why, I'm gonna knock you off of me."

"Fine." George latched on to Tank's hips, slamming his cock like a bucking bronco. He changed angles, making Tank holler his name. "That's right. Who's dick is in you?"

"Shut up." Tank thrust back, knocking George back with his ass and almost dislodging him.

"So, you wanna play games." George grabbed Tank's shoulders, lifting one leg and riding him like he was in a rodeo. Fuck yeah. He felt the tingling begin at the base of his spine. George reached under his mate, trying to get to his cock. Finally grabbing hold, he yanked along with his thrusts.

"George...gonna—" Tank's head fell back, his ass hitching higher.

"Give it to me. Give it to Daddy." George grinned.

"Smart ass." Tank growled.

"Thought you'd like that." He chuckled. "Or you can call me King George."

George stopped talking when he felt Tank's body shiver and stiffen. He squeezed Tank's shaft as he gave one more thrust. Tank erupted in his hand, his cock pulsing as it gave its creamy prize to George.

"Tank," George shouted as he slammed harder, lights bursting behind his eyes. Tank's muscled ass had a death grip on him. He fell onto Tank's back, heaving and sweaty.

"Fuck me, man." Tank fell forward.

"Just did." George chuckled as Tank tried to swat at him.

Tank pulled George over to him, kissing his temple. "You know you're mine. I won't share."

"Yeah, 'cause lord knows I've been beating back the guys." George rubbed his goatee against Tank's nipple, getting a groan from his mate.

"What about Kitty?" Tank shifted around to look him in his eyes.

"Uh, female. Duh."

"Okay, but I'll be watching her." Tank pulled George closer. He sighed and ran the palm of his hand over his mate's chest. The man had to have the broadest chest George had ever seen.

"Not too damn close." He murmured then yawned, snuggling close to own personal heater. George glanced up, seeing a mischievous grin on the man's face.

Tank smiled. "Jealous?

"You wish." So maybe he was, but that didn't mean Tank had to know. "Now be quiet and get some sleep or I'm gonna hogtie ya and put a gag on ya." George burrowed his head in the crook between Tank's chin and shoulder. If only he was this comfortable all the time.

* * * *

George whistled as he walked out of Tank's bedroom, but it died on his lips as a small tiger walked toward him. He could have sworn Tank said they were wolves. Maybe his mate was a little screwed up in the head and couldn't remember which animal he was because that was definitely a tiger in front of him.

George gulped when a large wolf came around the corner to follow behind the tiger. He reached up and rubbed his eyes, making sure he was seeing things right.

Yep, they were still there.

A hand landed on George's shoulder, and he swung his arm as he turned around. One of the warriors ducked and laughed. "Don't let them frighten you."

"Sorry." George cleared his throat, a bit embarrassed that the wild animals made him edgy. "So there are cats or dogs living here?"

The man chuckled. "Hi, I'm Loco. You must be George, Tank's mate."

He shook the offered hand, never letting his eyes leave the oddball pair walking slowly toward him.

"We're wolves. Kyoshi there, along with his cousin Keata, are tigers, shifters from southern Japan."

"Hope you don't think that explains it." George laughed nervously as he scratched his head. The small tiger stopped in front of him and sat back on its haunches. It batted a paw at him like a cat would do. Was that normal for a tiger?

"I think Kyoshi wants to play." Loco chuckled. George watched as the man reached down and scratched behind the tiger's ear, the wolf giving off a low growl.

"Mr. Cute and Fuzzy over there don't seem to keen on the idea of the tiger being touched. I think I'll keep all ten fingers if you don't mind." George took a step back.

"Nah, don't mind Storm. It's a mate thing. Kyoshi loves to have his ears scratched."

And the wolf looked like he'd *love* to eat Loco. No thanks. "Um, okay. I'm gonna go, you just keep on scratching the cat. Good luck."

George turned and walked a little faster than normal, putting a great amount of distance between his body and those sharp teeth.

He walked into the den, stomping over to the stereo and changing it until he found the local country station. His ears were gonna start bleeding in a minute if he continued to listen to that guitar wailing out that god-awful music.

"Hey, what the hell is that?" Cecil covered his ears.

"It's called music. Try it sometime." George walked behind the bar, looking for a beer.

"I will if I lose my wife or want my dog back." Cecil flicked the dial, putting his heavy metal back on.

"I'll keep listening to this if I want to commit suicide." George took his bottle of beer and walked back, changing it back to Garth Brooks.

"You want a shootout at noon?" Cecil placed his hands on his hips.

George bit back a smile. "Sundown tomorrow. Out back."

"Fine. Until then..." He swung the dial back to Metallica. George may not listen to the music, but he was up on the popular bands.

"Until then." George swung it back to his country song.

"Stop! I wanna kill my wife and lose my dog at the same time," Johnny yelled.

The stereo gave a loud buzz and then went dead.

"Now look what you did." Cecil glared at George then played with the dial.

"Me? It was that satanic music. Must have sucked out the stereo's soul." It took everything in George not to burst out laughing.

"What's going on in here?" Maverick walked into the den.

George and Cecil pointed at each other.

"He did it," they said in unison.

Maverick approached George, eyeing him up and down. "We haven't been formally introduced. Raiding the night club to hunt the mates down doesn't count. I am Maverick, Alpha of the Brac pack."

"I'm George, cook of the diner." George extended his hand.

Maverick's lip lifted in a smile as he shook George's hand.

"Another human with backbone. At least I don't have to consider killing you."

"Uh, thanks?" George looked over at Cecil, who was grinning.

Maverick laughed this time. "No problem. Welcome to our family."

"Hey, you didn't welcome me." Johnny pouted.

"No, Johnny, I didn't. Sorry. Welcome."

Johnny beamed. "Thanks."

Maverick shook his head. "Can I speak with you a moment in my office, George?"

"Sure. Just show me the way." George followed the ginormous man down the hall. Maverick waved him to a leather chair as he sat behind his desk.

"I know you're new to this whole mating thing and having knowledge of wolves and vampires, but I would appreciate it if you didn't let my mate, Cecil, talk you into another escape. They aren't prisoners here, but we guard our mates closely. There are those who would like nothing better than to harm or kill them. That includes you now." Maverick leaned back in his seat.

"I understand what you're saying and all, but if you don't mind me tellin' ya, they feel trapped. Maybe take them out once a month, twice maybe. Let them shake the cabin fever off." George shrugged.

"Good point. I'll take that into consideration." Maverick smiled. "I like you. You speak your mind respectfully."

"If that's all, I have a shootout with your mate soon." George stood and inclined his hat.

Maverick arched a brow. "Just don't kill him. He's mischievous, but I love him dearly."

"Gotcha." George headed back to the den.

* * * *

George crept around the corner, his assault rifle in front of him, ready to attack. He did a quick head check into the library. He saw that it was empty, so he moved on.

Entering the kitchen, he heard the static of a handheld walkie-talkie and the commands being whispered into it.

Dropping down to his belly, George crawled around the table, aiming his gun up. Squeezing the trigger, he fired in a quick burst, jumping up to run.

"Think you can shoot me?" Maverick yelled as George skidded out of the kitchen and raced up the stairs. He knew he hit Maverick dead on, wasn't a question about it.

Next he crept down the hallway, gun tucked to his shoulder, his eye focused in the sight as Keata came out of his room. George fired, hitting Keata in his chest.

"George!" Keata screamed, but he was already on the move.

The radio static buzzed again, and George tiptoed until he came to another room where Drew was hiding under the bed. George blasted him then ran back down the stairs, Drew screaming out that he was going to pay for that.

He entered Tank's room, finding himself face to face with Tank's weapon.

"Thought you could sneak up on me, didn't you?" Tank circled around him, nodding his head at George's gun, indicating he wanted him to drop it.

"I don't think so." George raised his gun, but Tank was faster, shooting George in his face.

"Ah, crap!" George ran from the room, heading to the den. Three warriors stood there with their sights on him, pulling their triggers simultaneously.

George yelled, dropping his gun and throwing his arms up to protect himself. Too late. George was soaking wet, water dripping down his hair and clothes.

* * * *

George jogged down his apartment steps. The day had been busy, and the kitchen was hot. He'd showered and was on his way to Tank's. His heart felt light. Tank made him happier than he'd ever been in his life. Just thinking about the giant made him want to laugh with joy.

He was humming happily as he made his way outside. It was a beautiful evening. Stars shone brightly in the cloudless sky. Love hung in the air around him. George chuckled. Since when did he start thinking so poetically? He grinned at the girly way he felt, and as cliché as it was, he felt like he was walking on cloud nine. The big goofy smile he was sporting was all because he had finally accepted who he was and who he wanted to be with. Speaking of, he needed to get to Tank's.

George whistled as he walked to his truck, wanting to shout that he was gay and how the big galoot was his. He had just reached his truck when he was jumped from behind, a fist punching into his kidney. His breath was momentarily knocked out of him, but he wasn't going down that easily. Whoever it was picked the wrong man to mug. George thrust his elbow back, but it felt like it hit a brick wall.

"Thought I forgot about you?"

George screamed as a searing pain tore through his neck. He threw his head back, connecting with whoever held him. Stars burst through his skull as he grabbed his neck and head simultaneously.

"Fucking human. You'll pay for that."

George felt his back opening up and blood warming his skin. He staggered as he grabbed a crowbar from the truck bed, swinging it wildly. It was the vampire from the other night. The one Tank had choked. The things fingernails were long, looking more like talons. He must have used them to rip George's back open.

The bloodsucker laughed. "Think you can beat me?"

"I may not be able to, but you won't walk away unharmed."

George grabbed the crowbar and plunged it into the vampire's chest, putting all his weight into it.

He knew he was battling for not only his life but time. The front of his white shirt was soaking up too much blood. He was bleeding out too fast. His pristine white shirt was being used like a sponge, and he could feel his jeans wet and sticky with it as well.

The vampire roared, knocking George to the ground as he pulled the crowbar free. "You bastard." The creature dropped to his knees, covering the gaping hole with his hands. He tumbled over, George kicking him to make sure he was dead, or dead again.

He knew that was one lucky-ass strike, to get him in his heart on the first try. It looked like the myth about wooden stakes was inaccurate. Somebody up there was watching out for him.

George pulled to his feet and staggered to the diner. He almost made it to the back door when he fell to his knees, his neck bleeding profusely and his back on fire. He crawled to the door and managed to get in, his vision blurring as he stumbled to the diner phone.

George grabbed a towel, pushing it into his neck to try and staunch the flow of blood, he grabbed the phone and dialed Tank's cell phone, he was getting light headed fast.

"Hello?"

"H–help—"

"George? George!" Tank yelled on the other end.

George slid to the floor, blackness surrounding him.

* * * *

"I need help. Something happened to my mate," Tank yelled into the den as he took off toward the front door. He wanted to shift, but what if George needed him to take him to the hospital?

Tank tore from the driveway, gravel spitting out and hitting the other vehicles. He made it to the diner to see his mate's truck. *Oh god, there was so much fucking blood.* It was splattered on George's truck and the sidewalk. Tank didn't think he had ever seen so much in one place in his life. The vampire from the other night was lying on the ground. Tank roared as he picked the body up and slammed it into a tree, watching it fall limply to the ground.

If he hadn't let the vamp get away, his mate wouldn't be hurt. Or maybe worse. Tank stormed into the diner, following the path of blood. George was slumped down behind the counter. His neck looked chewed open. *Oh god, no!*

He ran to George, pulling him into his arms, Tank howled when his hands felt the sticky blood on his mate's back. "Somebody help us!" Tank screamed as he rocked a lifeless cowboy in his arms. "Please, no," he choked out.

"Let's go, Tank. We gotta get him to a hospital fast. The Medic Center is close." Gunnar pulled at Tank's shoulder. He knew they had precious little time. George would bleed out if they didn't get him there fast.

"Okay." Tank wiped his eyes as he carried his mate in his arms, running him out the door and jumping into Gunnar's SUV. "Hurry. I can't lose him." Tank pulled his T-shirt up and wiped his face clean of snot and tears. He stared at the man lying lifeless in his arms. *There's so much fucking blood.*

"We ain't losing anyone tonight, buddy." Gunnar floored it, running every stop sign and light. He whipped the truck in front of the Center as Tank jumped out, screaming for someone to help him.

A young doctor raced toward Tank, pulling George from his arms. Tank fought to keep his mate with him.

"I can't help him if you don't give him to me." The doctor touched Tank's arm gently.

"Okay, but make him better." Tank let out a sob as the doctor wheeled him away.

The warriors came running into the Medic Center, surrounding Tank.

"What happened?" Maverick laid his hand on Tank's shoulder.

"Fucking vampires. Will he change now? Be one of them?" Tank hadn't thought of that before, but now it was the only thing on his mind besides his mate pulling through.

"I'm going to call Prince Christian and find out. Hang in there, Tank. He'll pull through." Maverick walked out to make his call.

Tank threw his head back and a howl ripped from his chest. It was so thunderous, the nurses ran behind the desk, cowering.

Gunnar grabbed Tank's arm. "Pull it together. I know you're hurting, man, but you can't do that here."

"Get the hell off of me." Tank yanked his arm away from Gunnar, slamming the front doors open and walking out into the night.

Chapter Seven

The mates sat somberly in the den, waiting on word about George.

"I didn't even get my shootout." Cecil grinned behind tears.

"He'll make it. We just broke him in." Kyoshi patted Cecil's arm.

"I'll listen to every damn sappy country song he plays if he pulls through." Cecil wiped his eyes. He had really taken a liking to the cowboy. The guy was definitely different and fun to be around. Cecil didn't even want to contemplate the possibility of anything happening to the man.

They all turned their heads when the front door slammed open. Tank stormed through the house.

If Tank was here, slamming things, did that mean…?

"I need to call Maverick." Cecil jumped up and ran down the hall to his mate's office, dialing with unsteady hands.

"Cecil?" Maverick asked when he answered his phone.

"Yeah, how is he? Why is Tank here?"

"We don't know yet, baby. But I'm glad we know where Tank ran off to. I'll keep you informed."

"Thanks." Cecil felt like crying over not having his mate with him at a time like this. It brought home how easily he could lose him. "Maverick?"

"Yeah, baby?"

"I love you."

"I love you, too."

Cecil hung up, relieved that Tank's appearance didn't mean George was dead. He made his way back to the other mates, their eyes questioning Cecil.

"They don't know yet."

"I thought…" Drew sobbed.

"Me, too."

* * * *

Jason looked out of the kitchen window. What the hell was Tank doing? Shouldn't he be at the hospital? He stepped outside, watching the manic movements Tank was making.

"Want some help?"

Tank looked at him as if he were a ghost. "I…yeah." The warrior wiped his tears on his shirt and began to clear away the brush. Whatever he wanted done, Jason would help.

* * * *

George woke up in the hospital, feeling like a bull had kicked him a hundred times. He reached up and felt gauze. There were bandages covering the entire right side of his shoulder and neck. His back hurt like hell, too.

"Hey."

George looked up to see Tank standing by the window, his eyes misty. Was his big galoot crying? "Hi." He gulped out his reply. His throat was dry, and all he wanted was for Tank to hold him. "Am I…?"

"Maverick called the Prince of the vampires. You won't turn. You may become thirstier and crave your meat a little bloodier, but no sucking blood." Tank walked over and ran his knuckles down the side of George's face. "How do you feel?"

"Like shit." George tried to reach up, but he was connected to too many damn wires. "Get this crap off of me." He tried to tug the dang thing lose, but it wouldn't give. There was too much tape holding it down.

"Can't. You need it." Tank stilled George's flailing arms.

"No, I don't. Now unhook me, or I'm gonna do it myself." He pulled the white thingy off of his finger, ready to snatch the IV from his arm. He was determined to get out of the hospital and forget being a victim. It was humiliating lying here with all these tubes sticking out of him. He was fine.

"Stop it. You need it. Do I have to tie you down?" Tank smacked his hand away. "There is a difference between being fine enough to leave and just plain stubbornness, and you're the most stubborn man I've ever met."

"Don't be abusing the invalid." George glared at him. George wasn't sure what those narrowed eyebrows meant, but he was getting out of here whether Tank wanted him to or not.

"You're not a damn invalid, just scratched up." Tank grabbed his wrists, wrestling with him to let go of the tubes. "If you don't calm down, you're gonna do even more damage."

"Dammit, Tank, I feel fine. I got cookin' to do." George looked pointedly at his mate. "I can't just lay here playing sick." George turned his head, not wanting the invincible Tank to see the pain in his eyes. He had thought he wasn't going to make it, that he would never see his Tank again, argue with him, make love to him or be made love to. He wasn't going to say all that out loud. He did have his pride.

"Seriously? You were attacked and bitten by a vampire, left for dead, and all you're worrying about is food?" Tank rolled his eyes. "You're unbelievable."

"Just get me out of here." George stopped fighting, his eyes pleading with Tank to take him home, take him anywhere else rather than leave him here.

"Why can't I say no to you? This is against my better judgment, George. You need to stay here and get well."

"I can get well at home just as well as here." George grinned. He knew he won this round. Tank may be a big intimidating man to most, but to George, he was a big teddy bear.

* * * *

Tank cleared his throat. "I'd like for you to move in with me." He grabbed the chair by the hospital bed and took a seat. A fight was coming. He could feel it in his gut.

George once again struggled to sit up. "I'll make you a deal. You smuggle me out of here and I'm all yours."

Tank's brows shot up. Was his cowboy giving in that easily?

George's head fell back onto his pillow. He was staring up at the ceiling as he spoke. "I know I've given you a rough time. I never meant to."

"I kinda understand." Tank stood and readjusted George's sheet so it fit snug around his body. He wasn't sure what to say. Was it his cowboy fighting as he emerged from the closet, or was it his sparkling personality?

"I've never been vain, but be honest, how hideous am I now?"

Tank sat back, his fingers tense in his lap. He prayed his mate wasn't going to fall into a depression. "You look like God himself kissed you on the forehead."

George stared chuckling, his eyes sparkling with laughter. He turned his head and stared at Tank. "Trying to get into my pants?"

"Trying to get into your heart," Tank teased. He was being serious, but George hadn't made a declaration yet, so he wasn't going to put any added pressure on him by saying the L word, not yet at least, but this was close enough.

"So, are you springing me or what?"

Tank shook his head. "You need to get better."

His mate narrowed his eyes at Tank. "If you get me out of here, I'll forget the scorecard *and* move in with you."

The man knew how to drive a hard bargain. "Let me see what I can do."

* * * *

"I can do it," George snapped as Tank tried to help him into their bed. He had finally talked the stubborn man into moving in with him. Tank agreed to spring him from the hospital if he did. He wasn't beyond blackmail if it got his mate in his bed every night. Besides, that tiny apartment felt claustrophobic. George needed room to breathe, room to move that fine ass around.

His neck healed in record time. Prince Christian said it would, and damn if he wasn't right. It looked like the attack never happened. But Tank liked taking care of him, so George would just have to deal with it.

"I know you can. Just let me take care of you." Tank tucked him in, sitting down next to him. "You scared me."

"I'm tougher than that." His mate scoffed.

"If you're tougher than that, come here." Tank pulled him up, walked George backward, and then hit the play button on the CD player bought just for George and his love of music.

"What are you doing?" George leaned back, his eyes searching. Tank would never get enough of looking into his baby blues. His mate was a spitfire, but Tank wouldn't have him any other way.

"You'd like to know, wouldn't you?" Tank grinned as he pulled George into his arms, and the melody began to play.

"That's Faith Hill's 'Beautiful.'" George gulped. "I'm floored that you know any country song, especially one so romantic."

Tank rocked back and forth with his mate in his arms, nuzzling George's neck. "I love you, George," Tank whispered into his neck. He knew he was pushing the boundaries by saying it, but it had slipped out as he thought of how close he was to losing his cowboy.

"I—I."

"You don't have to say it back. I just wanted you to know." He whirled George around, smiling as his mate laughed out loud. He pulled George back into his arms. "You mean the world to me. Never scare me again." Tank pulled him tight to his chest. The thought of never holding his mate again terrified him. He would hold the beautiful man in his arms forever if he thought the guy wouldn't curse him out for it.

Tank held him close, running his hands up and down George's back as the song echoed through the room.

"Wasn't planning on it." He danced Tank backwards until his legs hit the bed. "Your turn," George said softly.

Tank growled as he pulled George free of his clothes, stripping his own off in record time.

George dropped to his knees, looking up into Tank's eyes before he stuck his tongue out and licked the head of his cock.

"George." Tank moaned.

His mate parted his lips and sucked him in deep, palming Tank's sac in his hand as he licked the heavy vein that ran under his cock.

Tank ran his fingers through his mate's hair, encouraging him to take him deeper. George relaxed his throat muscles and took Tank to the base.

"George," Tank shouted, his hips snapping in an erratic rhythm. "Close." His eyes rolled back, the feeling overwhelming him. His body buzzed with excitement, knowing this was *his* George on his knees. No more one night stands, no more empty beds to wake up in. George owned him heart and soul.

Tank remembered the one-night stand from long ago. It was the night Cecil was kidnapped. The lonely feeling of knowing the guy he had snuck in wasn't his mate had hit home when the Alpha's mate had burst into the room. Thank goodness the guy he had brought home had been in the shower when the interruption had occurred.

Tank never had to feel that loneliness again. That ache one got in their chest knowing the person you were with wasn't your mate and wouldn't be sticking around.

George pushed Tank onto his back and jumped on him, taking him back into his mouth.

"Yes, George, yes, yes," Tank babbled as his mate tried to suck him through a hose. "Uh!" Tank howled as his release flooded George's throat.

"Fuck me." George grabbed the lube from the drawer, tossing it at Tank. Ah fuck, those words had Tank's cock coming back to life in a world record time.

"Impatient?" Tank readied him and slid home.

"Oh, hell." George went wild, he bucked back, slamming his ass against Tank as he grabbed his cock and jacked it frantically.

"Baby, I'm so damn close." Tank slammed his hands down on either side of George's hips and pistoned into him.

Tank's hands slid over George's cowboy butt, squeezing each mound. He had wanted to do that since first laying eyes on his mate. The tempting orbs had Tank ready to bite them.

His canines dropped, and his eyes shifted. He caressed the planes of George's back, his fingertip tracing each vertebra down George's spine.

He blanket George's back and lapped at his shoulder. Tank wasn't going to bite him. He fought the urge knowing what his mate had just gone through.

"Do it." George tilted his head, his voice quivering.

"Are you sure?"

"Now dammit, do it now." George bucked back, driving Tank to the edge.

He sank his canines in, and his brain exploded with the all-consuming flavor of George.

"Oh, God." George bowed his back. Tank closed the wound and yelled out his release as George wiggled underneath him.

"Fuck, I'm a girl now." George grinned as he fell to the bed. "You made me like being a bottom, love it now as a matter of fact."

"At least you're a good-looking one," Tank teased, curling around his cowboy and pulling him close.

"Shut up." George swatted at him from over his shoulder. "You tell anyone I said that, and I'll lasso ya to the bed."

Tank chuckled. "That sounds more like pleasure than a threat."

"That's 'cause you ain't right in the head."

* * * *

Johnny and Drew laughed as George threw the controller down. "How the heck do you fellas play this crap?"

"Is the game beating you?" Blair chuckled from the pool table where he and his brother were playing a game.

Johnny picked the controller up. "You have to try. You'll get the hang of it." He liked George and his big cowboy hat. He was funny and kind and didn't treat the shorter men like he was better than them.

George eyed the controller as if Johnny were handing him a snake. "It won't bite. Try it, please." He grinned when George took it.

"How do you play this dang game?"

"You have to shoot me before I shoot you." Johnny showed him how to use the controller. George grunted and then nodded.

"I think I can handle that."

Johnny bounced around in his favorite pink boots as he battled the cowboy. George was getting the hang of it, so Johnny had to step his game up.

"Oh, no, you don't, you little toad." George laughed as he overtook Johnny's man and killed him. The cowboy whooped while taking his hat off and hitting it on his thigh. "Gotcha."

"Beginner's luck." Johnny giggled. "You want a smoothie? I learned how to make them. Cody showed me." Johnny went behind the bar and pulled the blender out. He carefully counted out eight ice cubes and deposited them into the blender. *Remember to put the lid on before pressing start.* He repeated in his head. Next he added some strawberries and bananas, tossed in a few Cheerios—because it wasn't a smoothie without them. He kept a small bag of them stored next to the blender. Johnny grabbed the bottle of honey and carefully measured out one teaspoon, letting it drizzle into the blender. The last thing he added was yogurt.

Was that everything?

Deciding that it was, he placed the lid on and hit the button, listening to it whirl around.

"Looks good." George nodded at the spinning drink as he took a seat on the stool. Johnny couldn't talk. He was watching the clock. *Three, two, one.* He pressed stop and smiled at George.

"It's ready." Johnny grabbed to large glasses from the shelf and poured the smoothie into each glass. "Let me know if you like it." He spotted a whole Cheerio in his glass and panicked, glancing at George to try and see if his drink had any visible ones. He began to hum to himself as George drank.

"This is good." George saluted his glass to Johnny and got up. Johnny let out a relieved breath. He didn't know how to do the Heimlich if the cowboy began to choke on a Cheerio.

Chapter Eight

"Where are we going?" George let Tank lead him to the kitchen and out of the back door.

"No peeking." Tank had blindfolded him, saying something about not wanting to ruin the surprise. George held his mate's hand, feeling as though the world was finally right. It was scary as hell coming out of the closet for all to see, but with Tank at his side, he braved it.

"Is it much further, Papa Smurf?" George chuckled. He loved teasing this big bear of a man.

"Smarty-pants, you can take the blindfold off now."

George pulled the bandana off of his eyes and stumbled back. He had to be seeing things. *No way.* If he ever had any doubts about how Tank felt about him, well, this right here cemented it.

"I love you." Tank grabbed George around the waist. "You like?"

"Tank," George whispered as he walked toward the corral. Two beautiful Tabiano Tennessee Walking Horses were standing there peacefully. He reached out and petted one down her nose.

"I even built a stable for them. It's heated. I bought saddles and all that. Had an expert help me pick out everything we'll need to ride."

"I love you," George blurted out, emotions bombarding him. He could already feel the wind in his hair. "I...wow."

Tank cleared his throat, ignoring George's declaration. George was glad. He didn't like all that emotional stuff, but the moment was so overwhelming to him that it just came out.

"Ready to teach me how to ride?"

"Hell, yeah." George couldn't contain his excitement. He set the water container down that he had to carry with him now for his never ending thirst, but he didn't care. As long as the good lord gave him more time with Tank, he'd carry around a damn cooler for the rest of his life.

They rode the back forest, racing through the clearing, George had never been happier in his life. Tank made him feel whole, complete. He didn't care anymore who knew he was gay, as long as he had Tank. He finally understood Drew's words. Let the world suck a weenie.

Tank looked lost atop his horse but managed. George held his head back and enjoyed the sun shining down on it. *Was there anything more peaceful in life?*

"I think we should head back," Tank said after riding through the multitudes of clearings for a few hours.

George nodded and turned his horse around, guiding the beauties back to the barn.

They pulled the saddles and blankets off, taking the bits from the horse's mouths, and brushed them down. George showed Tank how to care for the gentle creatures. He fed them and made sure they had water. He made certain the temperature was perfect before he closed the doors.

"Thank you, Tank." George pulled the big oaf into his arms as he hugged him tight. "I'll never forget this."

Tank led him back into the house, George heading to the den.

"I believe *someone* owes me a showdown." George pulled Cecil up into his arms as he spun him around.

"G, stop it." Cecil giggled.

"Sundown, buddy." George set him on his feet, going over to the bar for a beer.

"Come on, G, play with me." Drew held out one of the controllers.

"I think my time with Johnny was plenty enough. I want to keep my record of one win." George swaggered over, setting his bottle down as he grabbed the controller from Oliver. "But then again, bring it on."

George struggled to race his car across the city and beat Drew to the finish line. He came in second, which shocked him. He beat the computer cars. Drew beat him, but George had fun. He played until Tank came and stole the controller from his hands.

"Hey, I was playing." George slapped Tank's hand.

"You do have to cook tomorrow," Tank reminded him.

"Yeah, yeah." George tapped knuckles with Drew. "Peace."

Tank stared at him with his mouth hanging open.

George swished his hips as he walked past Tank, pushing his mate's mouth closed. "You wish." He stopped swaying his hips and went back to his swagger.

"Not really." Tank followed behind him like a puppy.

* * * *

"Look, Kitty." George pinched the bridge of his nose, really tired of her coming on to him. "I'm gay. Always been gay, always will be."

"If you don't want to go out, just say so. You don't have to lie." Kitty spat at him.

"I ain't lying. I also know about all those rug rats running around. I ain't playing daddy to no one." George pushed past her, heading to the kitchen. This was ridiculous. Why should he have to explain himself? Weren't there laws against sexual harassment on the job? Some people just didn't know how to take no for an answer. Took it as a personal insult to themselves.

"Bastard." Kitty picked up a napkin dispenser and threw it at George's head.

"Get in my office now," Cody barked out, glaring at Kitty as he pointed to the back of the kitchen.

"I didn't do anything," she argued, crossing her arms over her bosom.

"Now." Cody looked over at George and nodded for him to get

back to work.

Ten minutes later Kitty came out, ranting and raving. "I'll sue you for this." She grabbed her coat from under the counter and stormed out of the diner.

"Looks like we're gonna need a new waitress. I fired her." Cody went over to the milkshake machine and made his mate a strawberry smoothie.

"I know someone, but it's a guy," Loco volunteered.

"I don't care, as long as he doesn't hit on any mates or mated warriors and knows what he's doing."

"He's a fast learner." Loco vouched for him.

"Bring him in. I'll see how he does, no guarantee." Cody leaned against the counter, watching his mate slurp down his smoothie.

"Thanks." Loco left the diner.

"His mate?" George asked.

"Don't know, maybe. I guess we will find out." Cody went back to his office as George headed into the kitchen. He watched the clock, excited about riding tonight with Tank. He thought about Jesse for the first time since mating Tank. His heart didn't hurt, and his stomach didn't cramp. Tank made him happy, made him a better man. George was proud of who he was now and the friends he made in the process. It was liberating not to have to hide. No one looked down on him, threatened, or kicked him out.

"Uh-oh. Tank gonna eat all food." Keata chuckled as Tank came through the door. George really liked Keata. A little girly looking, but his innocence was refreshing. Of course, trying to understand him was a challenge.

"That's okay, Keata. He gets anything he wants." George smiled as Tank wrapped him in his arms. "Love you, you big lug."

"Love you, too, George." Tank reached into the box he had brought in with him.

"Whatcha got?" George tried to peek past Tank's shoulder.

"Wouldn't you like to know?" Tank laughed as he held his hand behind his back. "Close your eyes."

"Why?"

"George, please?" Tank begged.

"Why?" George chuckled but closed them. He felt something being wrapped around his shoulders. Tank lifted his arms and pulled something around him tightly. "What are you doing? Better not be a bra." He could hear Keata giggling. Great, it probably was.

"Okay, open them." Tank stood back, admiring his work.

George looked down but really couldn't see what it was. He walked over to the chrome doors, staring at his reflection. "How does it work?"

Tank adjusted the leather straps. The contraption reminded George of a gun holster, but instead of a gun in the sheath, it was a water bottle. Thank god it wasn't a bra, or he would have had to have a showdown with Tank instead. "I rigged it so all you have to do is pull the hard plastic straw up, lean your head down a little and voilà, your thirst is quenched. Your hands are free now, no more carrying your bottle around."

George threw his arms around Tank, wiping his eyes into his mate's shirt to hide the tears. He wasn't no dang girl after all, and he wasn't going to be caught crying like one. "Thank you," he mumbled into Tank's chest.

Tank walked backwards until they were through the kitchen doors. "You're welcome. Now stop hiding those tears. Nobody in here but us."

"What tears?" George wiped at his eyes.

"You must be drinking too much water because it's starting to leak out from your eyes," Tank teased him.

"You're seeing things." George swatted a hand at him.

"I want to show you something after your showdown with Cecil." Tank pulled George into his arms.

"You showed me. I like it." George smiled into his chest. "No need convincing me."

"Perv, that's not what I was talking about." Tank smiled as he tucked his knuckle under George's chin, lifting his head for a kiss.

"Fine. Since you're not showing me your side of beef, what is it?"

"You wish. Just be ready." Tank swatted his ass before leaving his mate to work.

"Tease," George shouted from the kitchen.

Cody chuckled. "Harassing my employees?"

"Nope. That's why he's complaining." Tank grinned as he pushed the door open and left the diner. George stood in the doorway and grinned, watching his big bear walk out.

* * * *

"Ten paces then turn and shoot." George narrowed his eyes at Cecil.

"Make peace with Tank. You're going down," Cecil challenged.

"Backs to each other," Blair instructed in his sheriff's uniform. "No cheating."

"Damn, sunshine, you'll have to wear that to bed tonight." Kota growled.

Blair put his index finger to his lips. "Shush, I was planning on it." He winked at his mate before clearing his throat and turning to the dueling pair.

Oliver stood off to the side wearing scrubs and a medic coat, a black bag clutched to his chest.

"I think I'm having a heart attack. Check my cock," Micah teased Oliver. His mate rolled his eyes but blushed.

"Ready?" Blair shouted. The warriors were all standing by, the mates huddled around. Johnny bit his nails, jumping from foot to foot.

"Kick butt," Keata cheered.

"Just get on with it," George complained.

"Fine...now!" Blair called out, stepping back and out of the way as the two counted their ten paces. George's legs were longer, taking him further away.

They spun, and Cecil's chest exploded with colored lights. He dropped to the ground, his eyes closed as he lay there.

Oliver ran over and hit the button to stop the lights from flashing on the downed man's chest. He reached into his black bag and pulled out a sticker, slapping it on Cecil's head.

"Hey, what's that?" Cecil asked as he pulled the sticky paper from his forehead and looked at it. "Loser?" Cecil crumpled the sticker up, tossing it aside.

"I'm the winner." George jumped around doing a happy dance. He stilled when Tank came forward, pulling his laser tag vest from his chest. "I get to listen to my country music. I get to listen to my country music." George sang out his taunt.

"I want a rematch." Cecil pouted, mad because he lost.

"Baby loser," Micah shouted.

"Okay, enough teasing my mate." Maverick chuckled as he pulled Cecil from the ground. "Met your match."

"Nah, I let him win." Cecil pulled the straps off, holding his arms up for Maverick to pick him up. Maverick bent down, pulling his mate into his arms. "Come on, I'll let you win."

"What are we playing?"

Maverick laughed evilly. "You'll see." He carried his mate off as the crowd broke up, Micah swearing to Oliver that something ached on him and that his mate needed to give him mouth to cock.

Kota walked into the house with his hands held in the air, Blair pointing his pop gun at his back.

George shook his head and laughed as he watched the last of them enter the kitchen.

"Ready, Mr. Winner?"

George turned, seeing Tank standing there looking hesitant. His curiosity getting to him, he followed. What would make his mate look so uncertain?

"I want to show you something." Tank pulled him past the tree line, pulling his clothes off once they were out of sight of the back door.

"I told you I've already seen it, gorgeous, too." He watched as Tank revealed all his glorious skin. "We're screwing in the woods?"

Tank wiggled his brows. "After." Taking a deep breath, he added, "Now don't be afraid."

Nodding, George watched as his mate transformed into a wolf. Good lord, the wolf was the size of a pony! He wasn't going to lie to himself. He was a bit frightened. His mate was huge.

Deciding he could handle this, George ran his hand over Tank's wolf form. "Show off."

Bowing down, Tank lifted his head up to his mate. "Are you serious? You want me to ride you?"

The wolf nodded.

"I didn't bring a saddle." George teased but slid onto the large wolf's back. "No reins."

Tank huffed then stood.

"Don't go trying to buck me off."

Tank trotted along, carrying them deeper into the woods. George leaned his head back as he fisted Tank's scruff. The night was clear, and stars were out everywhere. This may not be the open range, but it was peaceful nonetheless. He could hear crickets and see small animals scurrying away.

He thought about Wyoming and the warm nights he'd slept under the stars, wondering how his life was going to turn out. Nothing close to this had entered his mind. He was a mate to a were-creature, and he was going to live one thousand years. That was a lot to take in, along with the fact that he now had vampire traits in him.

A far cry from Wyoming indeed. He shifted slightly as Tank walked over a fallen log, being careful not to unbalance his load. George ran his right hand over Tank's head, scratching behind his ear as he looked up at the stars. "It's a beautiful night, Tank."

Tank stopped as George watched the deer sniff the air then take off running.

"Bully." He chuckled.

Tank pulled his muzzle back. George knew his mate was smiling. They arrived at a small clearing, Tank lowering himself. Sliding off, George stretched his legs.

Tank shifted back, standing there as naked as the day he was born, and George drooled over the sculpted lines and muscles flexing as Tank reached out to him.

"You like it?" Tank asked as he pulled George down.

"Still think you need a saddle." He grinned.

Tank growled, pulling George on top of him as he lay on the ground. "Ride me."

"Ain't it your turn?"

Tank shrugged. "No clothes. I left my scorecard in my pants."

Rolling his eyes, George sighed, "I guess so."

His mate reached up, tickling him on his ribs. George fell over laughing, trying his best to scoot away. "Uncle!" he cried.

"Get undressed."

"Bossy." George stuck his tongue out but shed his clothes.

"Damn, you are one delicious-looking man." Tank patted his belly, indicating George to sit on him.

George stepped over Tank but didn't lower himself. Instead, he hitched his hips from side to side, his heavy and erect cock bobbing around. "You want some of this?"

"You know it, mate. I want to feel your tight ass around my cock."

"Keep talkin dirty, you may just get it." George's voice had dropped to a husky tone.

"Sit on my cock, cowboy. Ride me like a rodeo."

George's eyes hooded. "Close enough." He lowered himself, spitting on his hand and reaching back to stretch his hole.

"I want to watch." Tank panted.

George climbed off, turning on all fours so Tank could watch his own fingers push into his puckered hole.

"Fuck, baby, you make me want to eat your ass." Tank swatted his fingers aside, licking his hole, sucking then tongue fucking him.

"God, no one's ever done that." George arched his back, spreading his knees a little further apart. Tank slid two fingers in as he licked around them.

"Going to lose it. Better stop." George breathed out.

Tank pulled his fingers away, adding more spittle before lying back down. "Saddle up."

George mock punched him in the chest before mounting him. He leaned forward, guiding the side of beef to his ass. His hole opened wider. He felt fuller having sex this way. "Still not a girl." He moaned.

"Never thought you were." Tank planted his feet, grabbing George by his hips as he surged up. George fell forward, his palms connecting with Tank's chest. His fingers dug into Tank's chest, the thrill of the ride coursing through him. He leaned down and took Tank's mouth in a passionate kiss. Tank's fingers wrapped around Georg's neck and back, thrusting harder as George whimpered into his mouth. It was way too easy to get lost in the way Tank made love to him.

George broke the kiss and reared back, crying out into the night as he came.

Tank thrust harder, his back bowed and off the ground, trying to bury himself deep inside George then exploded. "George!" he shouted as his cock pulsed deep inside George's ass. Tank thrust quick bursts into George. Collapsing down, his arms fell to either side of him, spread eagle.

"You owe me two now." George smiled down at Tank. In his twenty-eight years, he had never been happier.

Tank filled that lonely void he hadn't realized he had until leaving his home state. Sure, he had messed around with Jesse, but something was always missing, maybe the fact they had to stay hidden bothered him more than he ever admitted to himself.

George rested on his mate's chest, breathing rapidly. Tank was still inside of him, not softening all the way. He took comfort in having a connection so intimate with his wolf.

Tank pulled George up, ready to slide free.

"Don't."

Tank nodded and skated his hands over his shoulders, back, and his hips. "Do you miss home?"

George turned his head sideways and stared off into the forest. "I used to have to sneak around, hide who I was. My home had wide open spaces and a horse I could ride." George kissed Tank's chest then stared into those deep brown eyes. "Now I can be who I want, no hiding. The forest has a lot of clearings, and I have a beautiful horse waiting at home for me. So no, I don't miss Wyoming."

* * * *

Tank hugged him tight, allowing his mate to squirm out of the embrace to look him in his eyes again. "I also have a really great guy that I know for sure will have my back and never deny me."

"You sure I'm really what you want?" Tank asked as he ran his hands through George's silky blond hair.

"Uh, fella, your cock is still up my ass. I'm pretty sure."

Tank ran his fingertips down George's face. "I was so afraid you would deny me. I wanted to claim you right there in the diner when Frank introduced us."

"I feel so special." He grinned.

"Do you miss him?"

George drew his brows together. "Who?"

"The man who broke your heart." It pained Tank to ask his mate, but he wanted to know, wanted to know if his lover was sharing his heart with another. He would have no choice but to deal with it. He wouldn't like it, but you can't help who holds your heart. He knew in time George would give Tank all of him.

"Jesse? Hell no, it doesn't hurt anymore to think of his betrayal. That's how I know I'm over him. Besides, got me a big galoot to love. No time for closet cases."

"Closet cases, huh? Gets claustrophobic in there I hear."

"Stifling." George brushed his lips across Tank's. With the romantic way his cowboy was acting, Tank was fully hardening again. George began to move around, pushing at Tank's chest as he rode him slowly. Tank hissed, placing his hands on George's sides as he helped him.

"You know where I lay my head. Feel free to grope me in my sleep anytime." Tank cried out as he came again, George tumbling right behind him.

"You can bet on that."

THE END

LYNNHAGEN@YAHOO.COM
HTTP://LYNNHAGEN.BLOGSPOT.COM/
HTTP://FACEBOOK.COM/LYNNHAGEN.MANLOVE

(Cody) Warrior timber wolf, big muscled man
multi Hair brown eyes

Keata, | Tiger Shifter Japanese man 5'2
Kia | Long black hair slender form

36-8 Kisses 1st
43-49 SEX claimed
63- 66 SEX
78- 80 picnic SEX
90- 91 Tiger PLAY
_____

george)human Cook, blue eyed blond
Cowboy. 6'3

tank) Sentry Timber WOLF 6'7

124 Kiss
136- 42 SEX claim
128 152- 55 tank bottoms
168 - 71 SEX

(Cody) Warrior timber wolf, big muscled man
multi Hair brown eyes

Keata,/Tiger Shifter Japanese man 5'2
Kia /Long black hair Slender form

36-8 Kisses 1st
43-49 SEX claimed
63- 66 SEX
78- 80 picnic SEX
90- 91 Tiger PLAY
_____

george)human Cook, blue eyed blond
Cowboy. 6'3

tank) Sentry Timber WOLF 6'7

124- kiss
136- 42 SEX claim
138 152- 55 tank bottoms
168- 71 SEX

CPSIA information can be obtained
at www.ICGtesting.com
Printed in the USA
LVOW13s1020150217

524350LV00016B/381/P